THE OUTLAW AND THE LADY

THE OUTLAW AND THE LADY

by

Chap O'Keefe

Dales Large Print Books
Long Preston, North Yorkshire,
BD23 4ND, England.

British Library Cataloguing in Publication Data.

O'Keefe, Chap
The outlaw and the lady.

A catalogue record of this book is available from the British Library

ISBN 978-1-84262-790-7 pbk

First published in Great Britain in 1994 by Robert Hale Limited

Published in Large Print 2011 by arrangement with Keith Chapman

Dales Large Print is an imprint of Library Magna Books Ltd.

Printed and bound in Great Britain by
T.J. (International) Ltd., Cornwall, PL28 8RW

1

Rebel Hell

It happened in the most desolate and mountainous part of Colorado – and it had everything and nothing to do with the War Between the States and the sacking and burning of a town in Kansas, close to the Missouri border, nigh on twenty years earlier.

That was the night Tod Larraby, then in his late teens but wise in and aged by the cruel lessons of civil war, learned he was running with scum.

The small, grey-clad troop to which he belonged had latterly been taken into the Confederate regular army along with the rest of the lauded guerrilla force celebrated by the civilian population of the South as

Quantrill's Raiders.

The fast-mounted Rebels surprised the Yankee sentries at the Kansas town's railroad yard, an important Union communications and supply depot. After a crackle of musketry and a flashing of sabres, the blue-uniformed opposition was overwhelmed and the sheds torched.

The mission was ostensibly accomplished when one of the Reb band yelled, 'Let's hurrah the goddamn town!'

The cry was taken up and the bloodlusting unit went clattering toward the lights along the straggling main street. Colt revolvers stabbed flame into the darkness.

The young Larraby, bemused, trailed in his fellows' wake, eating the dust stirred up by their horses' pounding hoofs.

Panic seized the already trembling town. Men tumbled out of their homes and places of entertainment. Some carried firearms and tried to pick off the raiders as they stormed through the yellow patches of lamplight. Not one Larraby saw succeeded and many were themselves cut down by the rampaging Southerners' indiscriminate bullets.

One reeling townsman, possibly a drunk, was ridden down under the stomping, iron-clad hoofs of a Confederate horse.

In the darkness, Larraby gasped. This was bringing needless death and destruction upon hapless civilians. And where was the glory in that?

Windows crashed in and a burning pitch-brand set a saloon afire. In seconds, it seemed, the place was engulfed in orange flame. An adjacent saddlery shop began to burn, and soon the fire was leaping from building to building.

Larraby observed a young woman, scarcely much older than himself, run out into the street, her skirt licked by flames and trailing smoke.

'Help me! Save me!' she cried, her shrill voice choking.

'C'mon, Quincy – yuh hears the girl!' a Rebel trooper shouted. He swung down from his horse and rushed to tear the burning garment from her back.

'I reckon!' Quincy, who'd been riding stirrup-to-stirrup with him, also dismounted and ran to help, while a third Reb held their loose horses.

Larraby thought that perhaps some sanity still prevailed among his companions. But to his horror the pair on foot continued to disrobe the girl, ripping at her petticoats and camisole. When she was buck naked, the first of them, visibly aroused with his manhood stretching the grey fabric at his crotch, unbuckled his belt. Covered by the second, who flourished his Colt at dismayed onlookers, he hurriedly took their victim in the dust of the street.

Then the pair changed places.

A protesting townie who dared to lift a Sharps rifle was shot dead.

All through the ordeal, the unfortunate girl screamed in fear-filled frenzy.

Larraby was sickened. The atrocity was inexcusable, even for the high-spirited young Southern gentlemen who'd flocked to join

Quantrill's irregular fighters.

And more was to follow. While Larraby slunk into the shadows secretly appalled, his hit-and-run band indulged in an orgy of thuggery and looting.

The Missouri-Kansas conflict predated the Civil War proper, but the expression of its hatred had been largely in barn burnings and the exchange of hasty shots. That night the riffraff in grey were brutal and murderous. They raised every imaginable hell.

'Savages!' Larraby muttered, his youthful, soft-whiskered lip quivering with outrage. 'No – worse than savages!'

He vowed that when the war was over, and whoever won, he would have done with all such ungodly escapades and their perpetrators. He would forget this apprenticeship in terror and blood-spilling and rape. He would put away his Colt .44 and walk the paths of civilization and peace.

But after the surrender at Appomattox things didn't work out that way.

The late-afternoon sun was throwing the purple shadows of the Rocky Mountains across the sprawl of oddly assorted buildings that was Silver Leaf when Tod Larraby entered the main street. He rode unhurriedly. At an altitude of nine thousand something feet, Larraby – a man feeling the chills of approaching middle age – was still getting himself acclimatized to the thin, high country air, and the trail he'd ridden to the raw mining boom town had been long and wearying.

But Larraby sat his saddle head high, undwarfed by his troubles, fatigue and the bleak backdrop of towering, near-bald crags that overhung Silver Leaf to the west.

He simply breathed a thankful sigh … and hoped. His bay mount shook its drooping head and blew a snort through distended nostrils, scenting the smelter smoke that cast an acrid pall over this new place.

Among those who observed the arrival of tired man and tired horse was town marshal Vince Addams. He saw the restrained lift of the tall stranger's chest when he sighed; he noted the width of shoulder and the lithe muscularity of Larraby's legs as he swung down from the bay and patiently slackened the cinch under the beast's sweat-marked belly. All these things had their eloquence. They suggested to Addams a man forced to run from some irresolvable problem, despite uncommon strength and capability.

Addams fingered the abundant black moustache that swept its wings above his hard trap of a mouth. Nothing was ever a sure thing, of course, and he'd need to play it smart. Not any drifter down on his luck would be ready to leap at what he had to offer. For a fact, most with savvy would be apt to turn him down. It was surely not a chore he would relish doing himself – which was exactly why he needed a prospect like this, a man who knew how to travel the frontier wilderness, who could handle trouble, but looked an acceptable cut above an out-and-out saddle bum.

At random, you couldn't pick a hombre better suited than the one he'd later learn was named Tod Larraby.

The stranger led his horse past Addams' office window, and the hollow-cheeked marshal drew back into the shadows. He didn't want to be seen subjecting the fellow to his narrow-eyed, searching gaze.

Addams saw a smooth-shaven face, presently shadowed with a maybe two-day stubble, set in an expression of granite hardness. Steel-grey eyes were coldly sardonic under the wide brim of a high-crowned Stetson. The odd twist of the stranger's mouth suggested an habitual bitterness.

There was also a vague familiarity about these features, and Addams wondered.

If his hunch was right, then a stroke of luck had come his way. Maybe it wouldn't be so hard to persuade this stranger after all…

Larraby was in the livery barn for a spell. He unsaddled the bay and pulled free the other tack himself. He saw the horse led into one of the stalls and gave money and orders for the twelve-hundred-pound gelding to be curried and brushed and given just so much grain.

These things he did with a care, but the hostler, who read men almost as well as he read horses, detected an absence in his manner, like it was a routine the new arrival had run through many times before in many different places.

'Stayin' hyar in Silver Leaf fer long?'

Larraby smiled bleakly. 'Depends. A man needs opportunity.'

The hostler appraised Larraby's clothes and his saddle. His faded garb suggested he might be a wandering cowpuncher, but his saddle, all creaking leather and battered brass, wasn't ideally built for working with cattle. It looked more like a cavalry saddle than a stock saddle.

'The work hyar's in the mines. Yuh don't look no part o' the silver rush crowd, mister.'

'I take what I can find,' Larraby said, his deep, soft voice still guarded.

The hostler's look slipped to the solid Army .44 revolver, stowed in the worn holster at the stranger's hip. He shrugged. 'Don't we all? As a youngker, I was a trapper m'self, but thar ain't so much o' thet hereabouts no more. 'Tain't good fur country that fills up with diggin's an' tents. Yuh needs it wild an' mighty thinly settled.'

Larraby listened, and said, 'You know these parts from way back?'

The subtle prompting got the oldster going. 'Why, yuh c'd still be a chicken an' know the old times in Silver Leaf. Minin' towns grow kinda sudden, yuh know?'

Larraby nodded. Transitions from mining camps of rough hovels to thriving modern towns, sometimes complete with gaslights and imposing opera houses, were characteristically frantic and often took less than a handful of years. During that time, the first men would be drawn by the potential for individual gain, but as deeper, more complicated operations were entered into, the work called for engineering expertise and capital investment.

Soon, populations would swell to tens of

thousands. Larraby knew, and counted on the fact, that not all the newcomers were necessarily miners or their dependants. There would be those who served the miners' needs and those who preyed on their weaknesses. Beside the refinements of churches, schools and libraries, thrown together with truly remarkable haste, would stand saloons and gambling halls and houses of prostitution – sometimes uncomfortably cheek-by-jowl as testimony to lack of planning and speed of growth.

'It's nacheral to forgit the town ain't no more than a mewlin' infant, less'n ten years born,' the hostler went on. 'First off, folks were crawlin' all over the mountains, tappin' most ev'ry outcroppin' of rock, scarin' off the beavers an' all sich critters. It was considerable bad med'cine fer them in the fur trade.'

Tod Larraby clucked sympathetically. 'Times change.'

'Don't they? Many o' my friends went broke or lit a shuck outa the territory.'

'So now it's the miner's country,' Larraby said.

The hostler scorned the idea. 'Naw … they ain't got no use fer the half of it! It's desolate land, mister, all canyons an' rock-littered mountainsides. In winter, when the snow comes, thar's no gittin' in or out. It's the back o' beyond awright. Hell, the minin' bosses done left it to the trash – the fiddle-foots an' desperadoes.'

'Sure sounds an unhealthy place!'

'Damned right it is, mister.' The livery man's bright eyes slitted shrewdly. 'Unless yuh happen to be ridin' the owlhoot trail yuhself. The hardcases've got theirselfs a dandy hideout up thar someplace. They call it the Camp. Only the outlaws know jest where it is. The lawman or bounty hunter thet's found it has never come back alive, that's a fact.'

Larraby frowned. 'Hmm…' he mused. 'Is this the hole-in-the-wall ramrodded by Jet Konaskis? Kind of a floating population of wanted men – led by a real ugly cuss with nothing to lose or gain? If it is, word has gotten outside this neck of the woods.'

'Konaskis … yeah, thet's the bastard's name. I seen 'im once. A big dev'l with a black beard down to his chest an' a harelip. Mean. God awful mean.'

'Ain't no sense in shoving on thataways then,' Larraby said with a nod toward the wide, open doors of the barn and the view of the mountains.

The old man trudged up to the entrance and spat out into the roadway. 'A body's safe to ride out thar a piece – long as he don't go to sniffin' off the main trails, I guess.'

Larraby hefted his warbag. 'Waal, thank you kindly for the advice, old timer. I ain't planning on moving on a-whiles, but I'll remember what you say.'

Wearily, slightly stiff-legged, Larraby went on down the street, past several false-fronted stores to a genuine two-floored brick building placed dominatingly where a cross street met the main. A balcony supported on carved and fretted posts embellished it at the upper level on the visible sides facing the streets. Lettering painted on the brickwork above the angled corner entrance bestowed the elaborate-looking structure with the high-sounding name of The Grand Hotel.

Larraby debated with himself whether he should look for more modest lodging. The weight of the coin in his pocket put no strain on studs or stitches, and his greenbacks were folded together rather than rolled. But what the hell … he was a lone wolf feeling his years. He hankered after some comfort. More, he thought ruefully; nothing less than a change in his position. Pursued by a reputation, he was sick of skipping from one range to another and needed an honest job.

He pushed at one of the big, oaken double doors and met unexpected resistance.

Intent on going on in, Larraby exerted more force. His muscle prevailed and the double-hinged door swung back. Larraby found himself standing face to face with a thick-set gent in a dark, three-piece city suit.

An ostentatious gold watch chain stretched across his barrel chest, and an unnatural flush of liquor and frustration across his mutton-chopped visage.

Clearly, the man within had been trying to come out at the same time as Larraby had been trying to push in. For a moment, the two glared at each other.

When the prosperous-looking hotel guest saw the low-bred stamp of the man who'd been blocking his progress, his frustration turned to simmering rage. 'Do you know who I am, sir?' he spluttered in an accent not familiar to Larraby.

Larraby didn't like his manner or the sickly fumes of stomach acid and whiskey. 'Can't say as I do. You could be any damned son – even the Sheikh of Araby his almighty self.'

The retort fired up the angry man further, but he took his temper in hand.

'Don't give me your lip! I'm Ralph John Sloan, the ninth earl of Buckhampton. Get out of my way!'

2

The Sad Englishwoman

Though his hackles were raised, Larraby was in no shape or mood to start a fight. He let the belligerent man barge on out past him. The accent and the title he'd given himself placed him as an Englishman, one of importance perhaps. He surely was important in his own estimation anyhow.

An earl, was he? Or so he claimed. An English lord out here in Colorado. Well, whom might a man meet next?

The lobby was proportioned and decked out on lines that bid to live up to the hotel's name. There were mahogany furnishings, a chandelier, deep brocade-covered settees and potted palms. But Larraby's eyes dwelled on none of these things.

His gaze crossed to the broad sweep of stairway leading to the upper floor. More particularly, it was drawn by the woman who had paused on the stairs to turn and look back, one slim white hand resting on the curve of the polished handrail.

She had clearly observed the exchange that had taken place at the door, and her interest lingered and was now directed to Larraby alone.

She was a fine figure of a woman, Larraby instantly thought. Fair-skinned, tall, deep-breasted – in every way a desirable female, probably in her late twenties. In a land where men outnumbered women three to one, she would be some proud man's wife for certain. So he was puzzled when the gleam of interest in her eyes persisted. Unless he was mistaken, due to some trick of the fading light, those eyes were the cobalt blue of a noon sky. They were perfect for her creamy flesh tones and the long golden hair done up in a roll and piled high on her head.

The meeting of their glances quickened

Larraby's pulse. This woman was more than a pretty face. She was quality – a thoroughbred. Teasing a common man wouldn't figure among her ways.

What, then, did she mean by her searching look?

She must have seen the questioning frown that furrowed his brow. Coolly, with a self-possession that told him she was a woman who understood men and was neither afraid nor silly, she glided down the stairs.

She wore an off-the-shoulder dress of regally purple silk which set off her comely figure to magnificence with its low-cut, heart-shaped bodice and nipped-in waist. The draped skirt fell in graceful folds to the floor. Her unhurried approach revealed glimpses of trim ankles and narrow feet.

'Forgive me,' she said, 'but I could not help witnessing my husband's regrettable boorishness.'

Her voice was mellow and educated, and very English. She sounded as though she was sincere in what she said. The few precise words were more than the mere apology good form might dictate. The regret, Larraby sensed, was deep and genuinely felt.

Larraby took off his hat. 'For your sake, ma'am, I'll take no offence.'

'I'm so glad.'

'You say you're married to that Buckhampton feller?'

'Indeed I am,' she said with a sigh. 'I'm Julia, Ralph's second Lady Buckhampton.'

Larraby could readily see how she might be a member of the English aristocracy. What he didn't cotton to was how she might have gotten herself hitched to a rude and aggressive codger many years her senior. She deserved a better man than that.

He sensed a conflict here that might well explain the sadness that lurked intriguingly just below the surface in her lovely blue eyes.

He dipped his head and gave her his best smile. 'I'm real glad to meet you, Lady Buckhampton.'

The woman tried a smile of her own. 'Julia,

please,' she said, a mite daringly for the times.

'My name's Larraby – *Tod* Larraby. And you've just helped me make up my mind to stay here,' Larraby said with equal directness.

'That's very nice – Tod. It will be a pleasure to have you as a fellow-guest.'

'I hope so, and that I'll be honoured to talk some more with such a fine person as yourself.'

Maybe his boldness and his compliment gave her cause to remember her position. She turned back toward the stairway, but there was no unfriendliness in her manner, just a hint of cautious reserve, when she said, 'Goodbye for now.'

Larraby approached the desk and rang for the clerk. By the time he'd shown, and Larraby had signed the register and been handed a room key, Julia, Lady Buckhampton, had gone.

He followed an ancient, bowlegged bellboy up the same stairs, pondering.

The young State of Colorado, because of its mountains and big-game hunting, had attracted tourists from its earliest years as a Territory with the same borders. But to Larraby's mind, the abrasive English nobleman and his beautiful but strangely sad wife were out of place in the rawness of Silver Leaf.

There were resort colonies for rich foreign folks – places like Colorado Springs, which had become a mecca for consumptives. Larraby had recently been there, skirting Pikes Peak, and had noted the mild and invigorating climate. The city had been founded on the treeless Plains less than ten years back by General William Jackson Palmer, a visionary railroad entrepreneur.

Maybe he would tell Julia about Palmer's 'Fountain Colony', and its celebrated medicinal springs at Manitou three miles off, if he got the chance. 'The one spot in the West where nice people could gather together and live out their days in gentility and peace,' that's what Palmer had called it.

Somehow, though, Larraby reckoned that beneath her cool and classy exterior, Julia had a captive spirit that was yearning to break loose like an unbroken mare penned up in a corral.

They'd spoken no more than a few words. Just pleasantries, in fact. Yet Larraby already felt there was a kind of special rapport between them, though he might have been deceived into thinking this by the natural softness of her voice.

It was tomfoolishness, of course. He'd no call to pry into her affairs or bother her with his well-intentioned advice. If it came to it, consorting with a married woman – a titled Englishwoman to boot – would be guaranteed to land a man like himself in a mess of trouble.

Also, he suspected that starting over with Lord Buckhampton anyplace, mild airs be damned, wouldn't come high on Julia's list of desires.

In a back room of the gloomy wooden shack

that was his home, Marshal Vince Addams pulled open a battered tin trunk and began rummaging through the contents.

Here was the junk and the memorabilia of a wandering life. He'd lost count of the times he'd pulled up stakes and moved on. The shuttling back and forth between Missouri and California had been almost constant as he won and lost elected terms as a peace officer.

Addams was the kind of man who used people and treachery was part of his stock-in-trade.

In among the old magazines and catalogues he tipped out from the trunk was a well-thumbed but latterly forgotten Bible. It fell open at *Proverbs,* drawing his darting eyes to a passage that had been marked by his wife. Tiring of his nomadic habits, this lady had walked out on him way back and joined a hypocritical, fire-and-brimstone preacher.

'Whoso diggeth a pit shall fall therein: and he that rolleth a stone, it will return upon him.'

Addams took in the printed words involuntarily, and scowled. His displeasure was mostly with himself for paying mind to such irrelevancy.

At last he found what he wanted – a sheaf of yellowing 'men wanted' handbills – and began riffling through them. He grunted with satisfaction when he turned up the one he must have remembered for ten or more years. The flyer offered a reward for Tod Larraby, wanted in connection with a bank robbery in Kentucky, pulled off by the Quincy Dunkin bunch.

Addams seemed to recall the Dunkin gang had later been broken up by Pinkerton operatives. The detective agency had been retained by banking interests to run down a postwar generation of hell-raisers who'd remoulded for bank and train robbery the technique of mounted hit-and-run raiding they'd learned under Quantrill and his equally evil lieutenants.

Larraby must have gotten away or been pardoned. But no never mind, this he could use as a lever of sorts. He'd fix some other way of plugging the loopholes. Larraby was vulnerable – at best no better than he ought to be, an ex-Confederate fighter too restless to settle down and undergo the rigours of being reconstructed.

'Once an outlaw, always an outlaw, I says.' Addams opined aloud. 'And it's *him* right enough.'

The picture on the handbill was of smudgy quality and showed a kid in Rebel garb. Addams' thin-lipped mouth quirked as he read the legend. 'White, male, age twenty, clean-shaven, grey eyes, brown hair.'

'Reckon he's aged a mite since then, but if he rode with them Quantrill hardcases, I figger his credentials for this have gotta be A-one.'

He took a last look at the young Larraby's brown-specked picture. 'I've got a job for you, Mr Larraby!' he said, his grin malicious, then he folded the bill and tucked it in a pocket. He tossed the rest of the papers back in the trunk.

His earlier estimation of Larraby seemingly confirmed by his findings, Addams congratulated himself on his luck and set out from his shack.

He'd put the first part of his plan into operation without delay.

Larraby was close to the bottom of the barrel financially. Any more than a few nights at the Grand Hotel would wipe him out. It was a sure bet anyhow that after the rigours of the long road he would have drifted along sooner or later to Silver Leaf's biggest and brightest saloon. Whatever towns had to offer men of his category in the name of entertainment, most of it was to be found in the saloons, with their liquor and percentage girls and games of chance.

Coins clinked fast on the mahogany bar and stakes were high on the green felt tables of the Silver Queen Saloon. There were velvet drapes and red plush seats. A polished brass footrail ran the length of the bar's front. At its back was a shimmering, ceiling-high mirror that seemed to double the size of the place.

A life-sized, gilt-framed painting graced another wall. Its subject was a nude woman stretched languorously on golden silk cushions; she had a come-and-get-me smile that could have made her the sister of any of the slightly more dressed painted ladies working the room.

Larraby bought himself a drink, none too large, and not wanting to swap lies about thrift with a sneering barkeep, eased on down the crowded room to watch the fall of the cards. Four tables of poker were in play. At another table, players and onlookers faced the dealer through a blue haze of tobacco smoke across a faro layout.

'Jack loses, trey wins.' The dealer, wearing a green eyeshade, slid the cards from his box and called them in a flat, droning voice.

Larraby's interest shifted quickly to the poker games.

A voice at his shoulder said confidentially, 'Highest stakes in town. Looking for a game?'

He summed up the man quickly. Tinhorn. A whey-faced, keen-eyed professional gambler dressed in a black Prince Albert, flashily embroidered waistcoat and string tie. Shrewd.

'Sure,' he said with a nod. 'Is there some place we can sit in?'

The gambler gave an oily smile. 'I'm kinda particular who I sets down with, friend. How about we make up our own party and take the spare table?'

Larraby shrugged his broad shoulders. 'Suits me if'n it can be done. Better than buying in.'

'You got it, feller.' The gambler stuck out a well-manicured hand with conspicuous fingernails. 'The name's Phineas Monk.' His clasp was soft and cold in Larraby's bigger paw.

'Tod Larraby.'

'You're a smart man, Tod. Poker's a game of mathematics and skill. Only fools treat it as pure chance. You gotta memorise the run of the cards, calculate a mite.'

Larraby hesitated. 'I ain't got no big table stakes, Mr Monk,' he warned.

Monk laughed. 'Aw, whatever you can spare will be just dandy. This'll be just a friendly game. We can work up from chickenfeed to the bigger stuff when you've raked in some winnings.'

'More like I'll drop out before too many hands are dealt,' Larraby said wryly.

A couple of off-shift miners clumped up to the saloon, the tread of their heavy work boots echoing on the sidewalk planking outside before they pushed in through the swinging batwing doors.

Monk winked. 'These boys are always looking for a game, and my – uh – associate Limpy Sikes can make it the five.'

It all came together neatly. Too neatly? Larraby didn't much mind. When it came to cards he was no greenhorn. He knew enough to spot, and not get suckered by, the exercise of illegal skills.

In a matter of moments the party was seated round the vacant table. Monk broke the seal on a new pack of cards and flipped through the pasteboards with his long fingers, inspecting them.

'All hunky-dory, gents. No flaws, no tampering.'

They cut for the deal and play got under way. Larraby settled down to match wits against wits, confident no sharper – should that be the true colour of Mr Monk or Mr Sikes – was going to fleece him.

Larraby aimed to stay in a while and for the first hour bet cautiously and held his own. He won a few hands, but unspectacularly – which suited him, because it was the small, regular wins which were the way to making money. Sometimes he miscalculated his cards' chances and held off when he could have raked in worthwhile sums.

Contrarily, the two miners, just paid, bet wildly, slamming fistfuls of dollars on the green felt, fattening the game and losing constantly but staying chipper.

The second hour was not far along when they elected to call a day.

'That's my limit,' said the first. 'I'm checkin' out.'

'Me, too,' said his companion. 'Lady Luck's robbin' us blind. I guess we're the losers.'

Larraby now had a respectable stack of poker chips and hard cash in front of him.

Monk said with a wave of his hand at the winnings, 'Your bets are coming off, Tod my friend, but I ain't aiming to quite less'n I'm busted... Your deal!'

Play resumed between the three of them. But during the next half hour, the run of luck seemed to change. Sikes, too, dropped out, and Monk began scooping in the loot with a vengeance.

Larraby's pile steadily and perturbingly diminished. Instinct told him something had gone oddly wrong. Tension built up, fed by his frowns and Monk's mocking grins.

'You're slipping, Tod,' the gambler told him. He spread a hand face up on the table – all picture cards. 'My pot. I figure you must be getting kinda used up. Can I buy you a drink?'

Larraby shook his head, both to say no and to clear it.

'This is more than the luck of the cards,' Monk said significantly. 'I figure you oughta watch closer – *real* closer.'

3

Gunplay in the Silver Queen

Even when Larraby judged his chances of holding winning hands good, and he knew he should probably win, Monk collected. Larraby grew suspicious. Was the gambler marking the cards with those sharpened fingernails? He'd heard once of a tinhorn who worked with a miniscule scrap of red dye under a nail.

But the shaded light and the thickening smoke would make such a trick difficult to pull here in the Silver Queen. Marked cards would be hard to follow in the gloom unless the marks were impossibly obvious.

What had Phineas Monk meant by his advice to watch closer? It had sounded almost like a taunt, as though Monk were deliberately daring Larraby to catch him out in some trickery.

Larraby kept his cool. He picked up and studied his new hand, his fingers untrembling, his brain still sharp. Only the reeking heap of cigarette and cheroot butts in the ashtray showed play was at an advanced stage.

He exulted, but didn't let it show by so much as the relaxing of one tiny facial muscle. He had three kings and two jacks – a full house. His memory of where most of the other high cards were in the never-shuffled deck told him it was an unbeatable combination. He pushed chips into the middle.

Monk glanced speculatively at his cards and raised an ironic eyebrow. He made no move to cast any dud cards he might hold and take better, fresh ones from the top of the stack.

'I'll raise you,' he said, pushing in double the number of Larraby's chips.

Larraby grunted. 'Suits me.'

He shoved in some more chips of his own to equal the bet. There was, to his certain knowledge, no way Monk could win. The only threatening cards he might hold from the part of the pack that had been dealt were three of the queens. Monk's other two cards would have to be number cards.

But he could understand why Monk was not trading them in.

The last card Larraby had dealt had gone to himself. It had been the jack of diamonds. He remembered that it preceeded a long run of minor-value cards before the next picture card, the final queen, was due to show up again. That queen must be halfway down what was left of the deck, neatly stacked in the middle of the table.

It also occurred to Larraby Monk would have figured out by now that he was a worthy opponent and one who would know more or less exactly where in the run of the pack the prime cards were figuring.

Consequently, he was amazed when Monk revealed his cards – *four* queens plus the joker, which could be counted as anything the holder wished, like a fifth queen, making it an invincible hand!

And an impossible hand, too, since the one joker, like the last queen, was buried in the bottom half of the pack and Larraby had naturally dealt off the top.

Monk was obviously up to tricks. He'd slipped in cards of his own – at least two of them – that could only have been tucked up his sleeves or somesuch.

But the most puzzling part was that Monk must be aware Larraby would *know* he was cheating.

The whole thing smelled of a stunt, but Larraby couldn't afford to let himself be cleaned out. When a man got wise to this kind of set-up, he was faced with a single, clear course of action.

Without telegraphing his intention, Larraby presented his own cards and leaned back in his chair looking up to meet the gambler's greasy smile. Then he was suddenly on his feet, the chair scraping the boards and crashing backwards.

'You cheating coyote, Monk!' he yelled. 'You've been palming cards! I say every red cent on this table is mine!'

The big Colt was out of his holster and filling his fist to back up his charge. He held it low, hardly more than hip-high.

Monk knew it was the way an expert handled his weapon and that Larraby meant business. In that vital moment he panicked, snatching inside his coat for a snub-nosed Derringer held in a shoulder rig.

He was fast, but the reaction was a bad mistake. Larraby had the drop on him, and because his immediate future had been riding on the game, he was riled enough to use it.

A sudden, intense silence had followed Larraby's denouncement. Most every tongue in the room had stilled and every eye swivelled to take in the grim tableau.

A woman screamed a millisecond before the two guns crashed simultaneously, viciously.

The black-garbed gambler had triggered before he could take aim. His bullet whistled past Larraby's head so close he felt its wind. It did Larraby no harm beyond a scare, but the framed nude on the wall got herself a neat second navel.

Larraby was no novice with a hand-gun. When the blue-black muzzle of his six-shooter stabbed flame, it got results. The heavy .44 slug smashed into Monk's gun arm, shattering the elbow. The double-barrelled Derringer flew from his nerveless fingers. He screamed with pain.

An uproar broke out.

Larraby barked, 'Steady, folks! We'll get to the rights of this without no more gunplay.'

Holstering his smoking Colt, Larraby ignored the ruckus and reached for the stack of undealt cards on the table. His eyes were like stone.

When he turned up the second joker to twin the one put down face up on the table by Monk, the excitement among the gaping onlookers rose to a fresh pitch.

Larraby's jawline tightened, and then his lip curled with disdain. 'Well, well well... Strange deck we've been playing with, Mr Monk,' he said.

'It wasn't my idea, Larraby!' the gambler gasped. 'Take the whole damned pot. You've done busted my arm. Lemme get to a doctor!'

Monk wasn't winning any sympathy. 'Twistin' bastard! He had it comin',' a red-bearded miner opined to a rumbling chorus of agreement.

Larraby said scornfully, 'Get out, Monk. It was a fool dodge, and I'm surprised. You must've known it wouldn't work. I suggest you light a shuck. No Silver Leaf folks won't be sitting with you at a poker table after this foofaraw.'

Groaning and ashen-faced, Phineas Monk stumbled away, supported only by his sidekick, Limpy Sikes.

'Damn that lawman,' Monk sobbed to Sikes. 'Damn him to almighty hell!'

Meanwhile, Larraby picked up the coin

and bills on the table. It was a tidy sum and he should have been pleased. 'But I don't get it,' he muttered. 'He was a professional – makes his meat with cards. He should've savvied I couldn't be done dirt thataway. It troubles me considerable.'

Card sharpers had all kinds of illegal skills for scalping the innocent, whereas what he'd just witnessed had been plain crude, like Monk had aimed on being caught.

It didn't add up at all.

'Hell! They've gone to shootin'!' Marshal Vince Addams' narrow face darkened. 'Either that asshole Monk's overplayed his hand, or the pesky saddle-bum's gone off half-cocked.'

Addams was loitering, but officiously, in the shadows off Main Street, close to the Silver Queen. He'd been waiting for trouble. Indeed, he'd been its instigator. Phineas Monk was acting as Addams' catspaw, eager to oblige the marshal in return for the promise of future favour. In the West, the friendship of a lawman was a mighty handy thing for an exponent of Monk's dubious art.

Monk's instructions had been to goad Larraby into causing a disturbance in the saloon. The plan was Addams would then have taken a hand, hauling Larraby into custody on whatever grounds could best be faked up.

The sound of gunfire put the marshal in a sweat. Dead men in his town didn't fit in with his schemes. At bottom, the whole purpose was that he should save himself a heap of trouble. Being landed with more of a different stripe was hardly to his fancy.

Grumpily, he stomped out of the darkness and onto the boardwalk, heading for the entrance to the Silver Queen.

Before he could get there, Monk and Sikes lurched through the batwings and came hurrying toward him.

'Quick! Quick!' Monk urged his partner. 'Get me to the sawbones – I'm bleeding to death!'

'What the devil's happened?' Addams hissed. 'You ain't gone an' killed Larraby, have you?'

'Shucks, no, mister marshal! But he's sure as hell ruined me. I can't play poker with an arm shot up like this!'

Addams was unmoved by the gambler's plight. 'You clumsy bastard,' he snarled in a low voice. 'Sounds like you've started pandemonium poppin' in thar. You'd better hightail it outa here. If I catch you in this bailiwick tomorrow, I'll hafta throw you in the calaboose!'

The marshal couldn't afford to let the gambler stick around and maybe embroil him in what he'd obviously turned into a foul-up.

Monk was in too much pain to be taken aback by Addams' cold-blooded renunciation of their pact. He blinked and grimaced before staggering on.

'The louse!' he complained bitterly to Sikes. Though Addams had proved a double-crossing scoundrel, Monk didn't have the strength to say or do more. He was a beaten man.

Sikes, the born follower, never did much of anything on his own initiative. 'Jail!' he whined. 'Shee-it, that'd be right unfriendly.'

Addams decided there was nothing for it but to push on into the Silver Queen. If Larraby had used his gun he might still be able to retrieve the situation to suit his ends.

In the saloon, the marshal shoved his way through the press of the rubbernecking crowd right up to the space around the tumbled chair and the poker table where Larraby was still stuffing coin and bills in his pockets.

Bodies fell back as best as those behind them would allow. Danger was in the smoky air.

Addams had drawn his Smith & Wesson revolver. 'I've got you covered, stranger,' he said harshly. 'Keep your hand off your gun.'

Larraby turned, his muscles like coiled springs. At the same moment, Addams was hauling the Colt .44 from his holster.

'I'd say you've got the wrong man,' Larraby said coolly, resisting the temptation to take his chances and lay the smaller man on the floor. 'What is this?'

'The law! D'you know who I am?'

Larraby squinted at Addams' badge. 'The town marshal?'

'Yeah. An' I ain't makin' no mistakes.' He sniffed at the muzzle of Larraby's Colt. 'You're the hombre that's bin shootin' in here.'

'One of 'em,' Larraby agreed. 'It was a fair draw. Let me explain.'

'I ain't swallowin' no fairy tales!' Addams snapped. 'I'm takin' you down to the jail-house. You can try tellin' your yarn there.'

He stuffed Larraby's gun into his own belt.

'It was Phineas Monk started it,' a by-standing teamster essayed helpfully. 'He got what was comin' to him. Nobody says diff'rent.'

'That's as maybe,' Addams said. 'An' I ain't sheddin' no tears over a two-bit gambler.

Howsomever, I don't see him around an' the law's gotta be upheld. This gent's under arrest for infringin' firearms edicts an' breachin' the peace.'

A buzz of conversation swept the place.

'Yeah!' Addams went on, raising his voice. 'It makes sense to check a drifter out. This one's plenty gun-handy, I reck'n. Could be he's wanted someplace – an *outlaw.*'

Larraby's jaw clenched. 'Now wait a minute–' he gritted. Then he shrugged and expelled his breath with a tongue-click of exasperation. He was in a corner here, for sure; best to go along with the bossy marshal. At the moment, there was nothing safer for him to do.

He let Addams drive him out of the saloon.

'You got good horse sense, I'll say that for you,' Addams told him with a sneer.

Larraby was escorted down the street to a stone building where a shingle hung out over the door inscribed: 'Office of the town marshal, Vincent Addams'.

'What's your name, feller?' Addams demanded when they'd got inside, though he knew it already.

Larraby had no lie prepared, which meant he didn't fall into that trap. 'It's Larraby. Tod Larraby.'

Addams nodded, smugly satisfied. 'Thought so. Wanted in Rosewell, Kentucky, for bank robbery. The murder of a teller there besides, I seem to recall.'

'That ain't true!' Larraby burst out hotly.

'Naw…?' Addams jeered. 'All outlaws say they're innocent.'

'My name was cleared,' Larraby said, striving to keep patience. 'I was completely exonerated. Quincy Dunkin, the real culprit, sought to blacken my name to settle wartime scores.'

'Is that so? Didn't you two fight on the same side, with them Quantrill hell-roarers?'

'I did, but I didn't like Dunkin's methods, an' I told him so. Afterward, I refused to join his gang, which made him sorer. When the war began, I was just a kid, mesmerised by the Quantrill spell – the spirit of adventure and Quantrill's dashing blond looks. Later, I noticed how spooky the man was, them heavy-lidded eyes hooding his cold ruthlessness.

'I also saw the murder an' the rape his men did against innocent civilians. I didn't enjoy watching. After the war was through, I tried to put that behind me. I never rode with the Dunkin gang, ever.'

'But you been on the dodge.'

'Because of Dunkin's goddamn lies, I tell you.' Larraby's voice shook with rage. 'I was denied a fresh start an' falsely branded a bank robber – a horse thief an' cattle rustler to boot. I've been forced to drift, but I came here *peaceable.*' He paused, his eyes flashing. 'Like I've tried to come to a lot of places.'

'You ain't never killed a man?'

Larraby sighed in frustration. 'When the bounty men've come hunting, I've had to go back to the gun, to stay alive. But I ain't on no prod. I want to be done with killing.'

Addams pulled the folded 'Wanted' sheet

from his coat pocket. Without sitting down or taking his eyes completely off Larraby, he spread it meaningfully on his desk, flattening the creases.

'I got my duty to do,' he said. 'I'm puttin' you in the lockup, Larraby. This has gotta be followed up. Thar could still be a rope waitin' for you someplace.'

Larraby nodded down at the paper, exasperated. 'That's old, marshal! You can see that.'

'Waal, yeah … maybe it ain't nothin' that'd hold up in front of a judge, but we'll see. An' meantime I got you roped up anyhow, feller.'

'How so?'

'Wearin' a gun inside town limits is against the local law; usin' it is worse. Duellin' is prohibited.'

Larraby laughed derisively. 'You can't enforce gun laws here! You'd have to arrest half the men in town if you were to try… Look, mister, I don't want no fight. I'll be happy to move on out of your blasted town.'

'Now, hold your hosses, Larraby! You ain't

lightin' out that easy.' He gestured at the Wanted notice. 'Apart from this, thar's a hefty fine mandatory for gunfightin'. You got two hun'erd dollars?'

'Course I ain't!' Larraby shot back.

Addams shook his head. 'Naw, not now you ain't.' He lowered his voice conspiratorially. 'But if you was in'erested, I might be able to fix it so's you'd have all o' that an' a damn sight more.'

4

The Proposition

Tod Larraby guessed then that the lasso loop had been whirling over his head from the moment he'd sat in the poker game with Phineas Monk. The unearned outlaw brand had caught up with him and dashed his hopes again.

He took a deep breath. 'What did you have in mind?' he asked Addams heavily.

'Nothin' illegal,' the snaky marshal rushed to assure him. 'Just a job for a feller who's trail-wise, an' can pick where a hombre might be apt to run when he's dodgin' trouble.'

'I ain't no lawman, nor bounty seeker neither.'

'This hombre ain't exactly wanted by the law, 'cept for questionin' over some minor thievin' an' suchlike. He's gone into the hills an' holed up, is all.'

'What's his name?'

'He calls hisself Johnny Lord, but we'll let that part keep for now. He's a hotheaded young buck an' he liberated a 'breed whore from a Leadville bordello, if "liberated" is the word. He kinda took to the owlhoot trail for thrills, takin' the 'breed along as his partner.'

Larraby rubbed his knuckles across his forehead. 'Why is he hiding?'

'The vice bosses in Leadville wanted him,' Addams explained. 'Same time he took the 'breed offa them, he set the bordello afire.'

Larraby raised his eyebrows and picked up on a tense. 'You say *wanted.* Don't they want him no more?'

'I guess not, seein' how his father has rebuilt the place for them an' paid plenty compensation to hush things up.'

Larraby grunted with distaste. 'Then if the law ain't bothered neither, who does want him?'

'The same father no less. Seems like Johnny Lord doesn't know yet the heat's off an' is still lyin' low. Pa'll pay big *dinero* to be reunited with his boy – a spoilt rich kid from way back.'

'Some doting father.'

'He can afford it. Well-heeled, you might say. He owns the corporation that owns the biggest silver mine in Silver Leaf. He likewise has huge ranchin' interests in the state, on the slopes to the east and south to Durango and the Trinidad Basin. A millionaire, sure 'nough.'

Larraby weighed it in his mind. 'Sounds interesting,' he said, his grey eyes speculative. 'I was looking for a job, and a rich boss with money to waste could be the best kind.'

'You know the choice,' Addams reminded him. 'For openers, I've got you dead to rights on this here saloon shootin', an' I got reason to hold you on suspicion till your record can be dug up.' He tapped the yellowed paper displayed on his desk.

Larraby disregarded the threat. 'Who is

this millionaire?' he asked.

Addams laughed dryly. 'You wouldn't credit it, but he's an Englishman – a real *lord* no less.'

'Lord Buckhampton?' Larraby said sharply.

'Why, yeah… D'you know him?' A shifty cautiousness crept into Addams' manner.

'Nope. But we met briefly, sort of, at the hotel doors, an' I spoke to his wife.'

Addams relaxed. 'That's all right then.'

'I hope so.'

'For your sake, it'd better be. To put it bluntly, Lord Buckhampton is a big wheel in these parts, an' he's travelled out here special. You don't cross him, see?'

Larraby nodded. 'I get the drift. An' you're not game to take the risk of failing to find his son yourself.'

Addams bristled, his black moustache quivering. 'Ain't that a-tall, Larraby,' he grated. 'Just thought I'd give you a second chance here in Silver Leaf.'

Larraby smiled sourly. 'Sure. So when do I get a proper introduction to his lordship?'

‘Tomorrow, soon as I can fix it.’

‘And how did you say I set about tracing his vanished son?’

Addams gave him a probing look. ‘I didn’t say, but I can put you onto a good lead right off – tonight.’

‘Go ahead,’ said Larraby, intrigued.

‘When Johnny Lord heard the Leadville interests were gunnin’ for him, he quit town in a hurry. He left his ’breed woman behind. She went back to her old trade at a girls’ boardin’-house, off lower Cross Street.’

‘You reckon she knows where Johnny Lord went?’

Addams lifted his narrow shoulders. ‘A man could try, but she won’t speak to no lawdog. Go to Madame Levanne’s and ask for Flame.’

‘Now?’

‘Feel free, but not too free – or I’ll put out a warrant layin’ unlawful discharge of a firearm an’ the woundin’ of Phineas Monk to your account.’

‘I’ll go,’ said Larraby with no great enthusiasm. 'I've got nothing to lose, have I?'

After he'd left, Addams chuckled to himself. The way he saw it, he'd been very clever. He'd snared a reputed outlaw. 'Set a thief to catch a thief,' he thought aloud.

Madame Levanne's so-called girls' boarding-house was not hard to find. It was set in an untidy cluster of jerry-built buildings down a gully, somewhat apart from the town's commercial centre.

Like in most communities of Silver Leaf's kind, the ratio of males to females was extremely unbalanced. It meant that less than a third of the men could ever expect to marry. Prostitution was inevitable in the cattle towns and the mining rush towns of the second half of the nineteenth century, and the authorities seldom attempted the impossible task of eradicating it. 'Respectable' Silver Leaf society tolerated Madame Levanne accordingly.

She kept most of her girls conveniently in her debt and therefore under her tight control, which suited the upright city fathers, if not the girls. The frontier prostitute's existence was a hard one. At least one of Madame Levanne's captives had taken her own life to end the misery. This had caused scarcely a ripple. After all, in big cities like Denver the week never went by when two or three shamed and suffering women didn't swallow an overdose of laudanum.

Tod Larraby rang the bell by a side door invitingly illuminated by a lamp in a wall bracket and was answered by the madam herself.

Levanne was a hard woman who bore the signs of her trade. Used to dealing with all conditions of men, she was efficient and straightforward.

'Flame?' she said, lifting a painted eyebrow; most of her time-ravaged face was masked with powder and rouge. 'You'll have to wait.'

'That'll be fine, ma'am.'

'Perhaps you'd admire a spell with another of my girls,' she suggested. 'There are five to choose from. We have Chiquita from south of the border, the Swedish twins Helga and Sussane–'

'No. Flame,' Larraby interrupted adamantly.

Levanne pouted. 'Flame is the best, of course. The price is seven dollars for ten minutes or fifteen dollars for a half-hour. The others might not be so much…'

'I'm not tempted, ma'am.'

'Well, she's worth the extra,' Levanne conceded with a sigh. 'And I can see her reputation is spreading.'

Larraby was led into a stuffy parlour where half a dozen other men were sitting. The windows were heavily draped and the air was thick with tobacco smoke underlaid with the smell of cheap perfume. He sat on a chair with curved legs and an overstuffed seat cushion and coolly surveyed the patrons.

The whore house attracted men of all types. From rich to poor; from the dandy in a frill-fronted shirt and Eastern-tailored suit to the down-and-out who looked as though he'd sold his saddle to be here. Some looked reckless; others anxious. But they all had the indefinable air of men in a railroad depot waiting-room.

One showed animation when a woman in a crumpled yellow dress came to the doorway and beckoned him. The dress hung from the swelling mounds of her breasts, beginning just above the nipples, and its short skirt was slit at the sides to show an expanse of creamy thigh. But the smile on her red lips was as artificial as the colour. She had dark rings around her eyes and her mouse-brown hair was stringy and lank as though she'd been engaged in sweaty work, which, Larraby surmised, she probably had.

Flame was something else.

Larraby saw instantly why a man wouldn't mind waiting for her. Just looking at her sent the blood pounding hotly through his arteries. Slim and statuesque, with dusky skin, brilliant brown eyes and raven-dark hair, she oozed sexuality.

A half-hour later, he followed her up

creaking stairs to a barely-furnished room dominated by a brass-railed bed. A tall red candle burned smokily on a wooden wash-stand.

The young woman slipped sinuously out of a filmy red wrap and let down her hair in a sin-black cascade.

'Flame…' Larraby murmured, appreciating the splendid proportions of her long, smooth-skinned legs and hour-glass body. 'It sure fits … but you must have a real name?'

She laughed. 'I'm the daughter of a Ute Indian and a white woman, stranger. My other name is unpronounceable to your race. I abandoned it with my virginity.'

That figured, too. She wouldn't need encumbrances that could indelicately remind some of the clients who bedded her they were that close to playing out the part of a despised squawman. It might detract from the assets that would have been her best meal-ticket since puberty.

Larraby could imagine how the blooming

half-breed would have embraced sex as she discovered it freed her from a childhood undoubtedly marked by tensions and deprivation, if not rejection.

He nodded, eyeing her body with the same frankness with which she exposed it. He didn't want to arouse her suspicions by seeking information too eagerly. Besides, it was pleasurable enough to watch her. Why spoil it if he didn't have to?

'Your ancestry doesn't bother me,' he confirmed to her, knowing that by her admission of it she'd already assumed that. To her he was just another transient no doubt – a tumbleweed, a saddle tramp.

It didn't make him feel too good, knowing a mining-town whore, no matter how alluring, could sum him up so readily. Could see he was of no account at an age when his fortunes, like his physical frame, should be in their prime.

Flame's slender brown fingers went to release the tight lacing at the front of the red camisole which pushed up her sculpted breasts. She let her hands brush against her nipples, making them more prominent beneath the satiny fabric. Then she paused.

'Perhaps you would want to undress me yourself?' she said, making it a question.

Larraby didn't deny it. He knew also that to reject the invitation would seem odd indeed. 'That and everything else,' he said with a natural honesty. He reached out.

His hands hovered for a moment before they thrust inside the loosened garment, pushing it adrift and revealing her breasts. He covered them next instant, his cupping palms gently lifting and taking the vibrant weight. Hard buttons of nipples burgeoned tautly against the caress of his roughened skin.

A tingling current seemed to race up his arms and through his trunk to his groin.

She laughed again musically, knowingly.

Well, thought Larraby, she found pleasure in her work, or she dissembled well. Knowing his own needs, he wondered if her belly was likewise filling with a pleasant dull ache that begged for release.

Maybe not. She would have long grown accustomed to being used hastily by rough miners and hypocritical townsmen intent on their own gratification and to hell with the feelings of a whore.

With lazy grace, Flame freed herself and ran her hands down her sides, peeling off her only remaining clothing. Where the scanty red triangle of her Parisian underwear had been was left a glistening pubic blackness. The knickers drifted on down her bronze legs to her ankles.

She was conscious and proud of her body and the effect it had on men. Satisfaction glinted in the dark pools of her eyes as she noted Larraby's wordless stare.

'You see everything as you would like it,' she said, with a toss of her head. 'Now I will show you what it is to touch and feel. I will make it like a drug. You will want to come again and again.'

She stepped out of the pool of fabric at her feet and put her arms round Larraby's neck and entwined him like a petted cat coiling its tail around a holder's arm.

Larraby didn't try to pull away, but let her draw him down with her as she rolled onto the bed, spreading her legs to each side of his own and taking his weight on top of her.

Her deft hands became busy with the metal buttons at the front of his denims.

He had no call to fake. Neither of them had to spell anything out with clumsy words. He would do this because it was expected. It was appropriate. And it was what at this moment he most acutely wanted.

Whore … 'breed … label her what you liked, Flame was a whole helluva lot of woman.

Impatiently, he knelt up and pulled the pants away. His thrusting manhood sprang free. 'We'll do this properly,' he said with warmth, controlling his urge to throw himself back onto her inviting body.

He sat on the edge of the bed and yanked off his boots and the rest of his clothes.

She purred, Larraby thought approvingly.

When he returned to her, she took a fondling grip on him, her fingers cool against the heat of his hardened flesh. Then she arched her back as he lowered himself over her and her hands moved up behind his broad shoulders, leaving his thrust to find its own unerring path.

Her supple body accommodated him, like a well-oiled lock might take a key.

5

'No Place for Greenhorns'

Larraby disengaged himself from their limp, panting embrace, breaking the union. His body was still aroused and he knew he had the desire and the capacity to pleasure Flame again, but he could not let himself forget he had another purpose here besides the satisfaction she had given him.

How did he raise the subject?

It had been good between them. He did not like the idea of antagonizing her now by blundering into heavy-handed questions. The soft moans of her ecstasy still echoed in his brain, and he knew she'd not been play-acting. On both sides, there had been an urgency and release in their intercourse.

In the event, Flame gave him the opportunity he needed to make his inquiries.

'You come back sometime,' she said, after a long, sated sigh.

Larraby, pulling on his pants, his senses still giddy, grunted a maybe.

Flame leaned forward. Her full, sweat-soaked breasts, the nipples still erect, brushed his arm. Her lustrous dark hair swept his cheek. She kissed his bare shoulder cajolingly.

'I'll do it for a special price,' she said. 'The madam doesn't have to know.'

'Tell me,' Larraby said, 'hasn't a girl like you got a regular man? What are you doing working for this Levanne woman?'

Flame dropped her eyes. 'There *is* a man – a very exciting man, but you must not make me brood about him. And a girl has her living to earn the best way she can.'

'Who is this man?'

'They call him Johnny Lord and he has many enemies, my friend.' She laughed tinklingly at remembered amusement. 'He burned down the bordello where I worked in Leadville. It was almost a jape to him, you understand?'

'Only sort of.'

'He lives for daredevilry, it's his way,' she said boastfully. 'But now powerful men hunt him, so he has gone into the mountains for a spell, to escape their anger.'

Larraby frowned. 'That's mighty inhospitable country. How will he make out up there?'

'He will join the outlaws at the famous Camp. My Johnny has a big reputation for lawlessness,' she bragged. 'Jet Konaskis, the robber czar himself, will be happy to recruit him. He will be welcome and safe there.'

'Is that so?'

'Of course! Johnny is very clever. He has many plans. Like how to steal the silver from the bullion train–' She broke off, as though sensing she was saying too much in the weak-headedness that had followed her exertions. The man with her was a stranger. Their intimacy was of a physical and professional kind.

Larraby nodded, but didn't press her with more questions. He arose and went to leave, silently. Let her think he felt slighted by her praises of the magnificent Johnny. It would be better that way.

'You will come back, won't you?' she called seductively after his departing back as he went down the creaking stairs.

Outside, despite the late hour, an ore-reducing mill filled the lower reaches of the barren gully with the steady throbbing of the stone-crushing stamps.

So Johnny Lord had ridden out for the notorious Camp to join Jet Konaskis!

Larraby cast his mind back to the words he'd had with the hostler at the livery stable on his arrival in Silver Leaf. The canyon country was dangerous territory. No lawman who'd ridden in search of Konaskis' hideout had ever come back alive. Small wonder Marshal Vince Addams had gone to such lengths to depute the quest for the English peer's runaway son. And small wonder he'd mentioned neither the Camp nor Konaskis.

Larraby had a shrewd idea Addams had known from the outset what he would be letting him in for. Momentarily, he considered whether he should cut and run. Then he pushed the temptation away. He'd done enough running and suffered enough harassment by the law to know that being a fugitive was what, above all else, he wanted to be shot of. He wanted to be done with the shootouts and the killing…

Maybe it wouldn't be so bad. He carried the outlaw brand himself. When he'd located the hangout, he'd give Konaskis and his bunch no cause for argument. He'd sue for acceptance as one of their own. And he'd stick strictly to the business of getting the hotheaded Johnny Lord back to his grateful father.

Then the slate for himself would be clean.

The distant rhythmical thud of machinery went relentlessly on. The mills and the smelting works filled the district with din and smoke all of the day and all of the night.

Larraby let his eyes lift from the lighted bustle of the streets to the dark, hulking mass of the broken timber lands beyond. Both had their dangers for him, it seemed. He'd tackled the one and fallen foul of a scheming lawman. Now the mountains beckoned.

He didn't reckon it would be only serenity and nature's wonders waiting for him in that wilderness.

Lord Buckhampton belched and tossed his bombshell across the lunch table. 'I'll be going along with you, Mr Larraby.'

Tod Larraby did a double-take. 'Into the mountains?'

The nobleman dabbed at his whiskers with a table napkin. 'Wherever else do y'think I meant, fool?' he growled.

'Uh-uh,' Larraby objected, shaking his head. 'That's no place for greenhorns, sir. Seasoned frontiersmen have come back feet-first, or not at all. I'll travel alone – fast an' light. I won't come back without Johnny Lord – your son, Lord John Sloan, that is – and if I run into trouble, I'll send word back to you somehow, unless I get killed.'

Buckhampton was not used to contradiction. 'Blast it all, man, I said I'm coming, didn't I? And I'll pay for all the equipment needed. We'll take the very best.'

Larraby went to rise to his feet, protesting, but Addams stayed him with a bony-fingered clutch around his forearm. 'Lord Buckhampton is the *boss,* Larraby. You want this thing to run smooth, don't yuh?' he said warningly.

'I won't sleep restfully until I see my boy again,' Buckhampton grated. The distant look in his eyes wasn't entirely due to the liberal quantity of whiskey he'd consumed – it told Larraby he wasn't quite sane about the matter.

Larraby snorted. 'Aw … hell!' he said under his breath, accepting the situation with a shrug. He picked up his glass.

'And another thing,' Buckhampton went

on, bringing his gaze back to the small group at the table and in particular to its last member, the beautiful Julia. 'My wife will come with us, too.'

Larraby usually took a care to moderate his language in mixed and polite company, but this time he couldn't help himself. 'She-it!' he spluttered into his beer. Immediately conscious of his lapse, he coloured and dipped his head toward Julia. 'Beg pardon, ma'am, but it'd be plumb crazy taking a lady along. There's hoodlums an' terrorists up there, an' they ain't no respecters of women-folk.'

Julia lifted her golden head and threw Larraby a blue-eyed look full of resignation and sympathy.

'My husband is a strong-willed man, Mr Larraby,' she said, giving the words a wealth of meaning.

Julia brought to the table an air of distinction. The effect of her white skin was very becoming against the plain blue of a gown trimmed at collar and cuff with lace. She was dressed, Larraby thought, for the Palm Court in San Francisco's Palace Hotel rather than a mining town in Colorado.

Larraby determined to press his argument despite Addams' dirty looks.

He said gravely to the table at large, 'No offence, but the last needful thing on a dangerous trip is she-male persons getting underfoot an' crowding the elbow of a feller's gun arm. Lady Buckhampton will be safer here, in civilization.'

Buckhampton's face reddened. 'Tcah! You call this civilisation?'

'Waal, maybe the lady could be sent to Leadville. That's a real metropolis.'

Larraby noticed Julia was shaking her head at him, but he tried to ignore her attempt at communication. On several occasions during the meal he'd caught her looking at him with an intensity of interest that made him uneasy. Again, he found himself conjecturing about the relationship between her and her aggressive husband. Because it was not the time for it, he forced himself to rein in his racing thoughts.

'Bull!' said Buckhampton. 'Leadville's primitive – another mining-town dump full of ruffians!'

Larraby was on the point of saying Leadville housed fifteen thousand souls, had thirtysome miles of streets, gas light, a water works, thirteen schools, five churches and three hospitals. But he bit his tongue. Buckhampton would be as aware of these statistics as any active investor, and clearly they cut no ice.

'Julia goes where I can keep my own eye on her,' Buckhampton went on firmly.

'What in hell for?' Larraby had to ask.

Buckhampton thumped the table with a clenched fist. 'I delegate her protection to no one! Leave her nowhere! I'll hear no more nonsense about *that,* d'you understand?'

Larraby grimaced and nodded, yet he had no illusions. The trail would be hard for anyone, let alone a genteel Englishwoman. He was horrified by Buckhampton's unfeeling stupidity; his blinding, fierce possessiveness, if that's what it actually was.

'So be it,' he said unhappily. He wanted to add, 'Anything happens to her, it won't be my fault.' But he thought better of it.

He could only trust that the hidden character he'd glimpsed before in Julia signified a lashing of strength in adversity.

Larraby was a born and bred Westerner. He knew that even the frailest-looking of women – which Julia was not – could draw on unexpected reserves of ability and courage. The record books testified to it with the stories of pioneer women from the Old World who'd defied expectation in going against some very heavy odds indeed.

He hoped if the testing came it would prove that way with Julia.

It was as well this wasn't winter. A trek with two tenderfeet into the Rockies then would be suicide. Snow and ice would obliterate the dim trails, making the going treacherous for man and horse. Freezing winds would cut to the bone. Blinding blizzards would make progress tedious and sometimes impossible through the high passes.

Even so, the mountains had year-round frosts. The sun might be hot during the day, but the mercury hovered near freezing-point every night of the short summer.

Larraby spent the afternoon buying the stuff he knew they would need. He decided to take three pack-horses – two to carry their bedrolls, extra blankets and quilts, and a third loaded with camping rig. Buckhampton had given him a thick roll of greenbacks, but he found the merchants in Silver Leaf, once they knew whom he was acting on behalf of, would have willingly extended credit anyhow. The English financier's name had clout here. He was confident his own hunting skills would at this time of year, and in this country, provide them with fresh meat and fish on the journey. But he bought coffee and bacon, sacks of dried beans and flour, baking powder, a block of salt, and enough baked bread for three days. Buckhampton's instructions were that the expedition was to be 'well-found' but not luxurious.

He also procured pots, pans, a Dutch oven, eating utensils and tin plates and mugs.

The trek was going to be no picnic.

The ordeal Julia would be facing preyed on his mind constantly while he searched out the best mounts and goods available. It was thinking of her comfort that prompted him to add a quantity of tea, sugar, raisins and butter to the provisions.

At the appointed hour of four he reported back to Lord Buckhampton in the harness room back of the livery stable where it was arranged the equipment would be stored till their planned departure at sun-up next day.

Buckhampton had brought along Julia, and it was to her Larraby proudly displayed the saddle he'd procured for her use – a velvet-covered side-saddle with almost no horn.

'Ridiculous!' Buckhampton snapped. 'Julia's a competent horsewoman and will ride cavalier fashion like any man. There'll be no deference to colonial prejudice, I tell you!'

The peer had been drinking and his words were slightly slurred.

Julia, maybe conscious of Larraby's embarrassment at her husband's outburst, favoured him with a sympathetic smile. But Larraby also glimpsed a flicker of wry amusement in her eyes.

'My lord is right, Mr Larraby,' she said. 'It really would be painfully slow travel if I had to ride any great distance in the conventional Western mode.'

Larraby was puzzled as to how she might dress for the ride. Would she cast aside her skirts and don masculine dress? This, too, would be unwonted fashion in these parts – an impropriety apt to cause astonishment and disrespect.

Given Buckhampton's tetchiness, he quickly decided not to pursue the subject. 'I'll swop it for a Mexican saddle,' he promised gruffly with a shrug.

'Too right you will!' Buckhampton said,

glaring. 'I'll not have you wasting my money on any damned nonsense, let that be understood!'

Another smile pulled at the corner of Julia's delectable lips. She seemed relieved Larraby had let Buckhampton have his way. Larraby was hefting the side-saddle clear of the other rig. As she left in her husband's wake, the woman let her fingers trail across the back of the outlaw's hand.

'Thank you,' she whispered to him.

Larraby wondered if Julia knew what she and her bullying husband were letting her in for, tackling the wilderness. If she did, he admired her coolness and guts.

6

Night Developments

Julia was no fool. She was long resigned to humouring her jealous second husband's whims, but she had no illusions about what lay ahead of her.

Out on the trail into the Rockies, anything could happen. Discounting accidents and the elements, they could meet up with wolves, grizzlies, mountain cats. Most unpredictable would be enemies of the two-legged kind, resenting intrusion into their mountain fastness.

But Julia knew there was nothing she could do but wait for sun-up, set out with her husband and their guide, and see what would happen. And pray to God that the worst didn't.

If any comfort was to be found in the situation, it was that the man who'd somehow been tricked into serving them exuded an air of good sense and honesty. He was strong and able. She'd noticed right off, when she'd first sighted him, that he was a fine physical specimen of manhood, perfectly co-ordinated and thankfully of a steady temper. A man rash enough to let himself be provoked by Ralph's ugly manners would have been the worst sort of companion in their quest.

But Tod Larraby, she sensed, would know how to look after himself and his party if any man would. She had watched the way he had brought the horses into the stable. He was good with animals, kind but firm, good-natured but not too tolerant. And the way he handled himself, she had seen before, was calm and self-confident.

Back in their rooms at the Grand Hotel, her husband dragged a carpet-bag from under the bed. It clanked and Julia guessed immediately it was packed with bottles.

Whiskey bottles. Full ones.

'Oh no!' she cried involuntarily and on a note of despair. 'We're not toting that load with us, are we?'

'Shut your trap, wife! I'll take what I fancy to keep me warm.'

'Can't you make do with more clothes, like I will?' she said spunkily, not caring to veil her contempt. 'And Mr Larraby, I'm sure *he* won't soak himself in strong liquor.'

Buckhampton sneered. 'Of course he won't. I won't let him! Besides, you and he won't need anything extra to keep your blood running hot.'

Julia was startled. 'What do you mean?'

'I've seen the flush on the fool's face when he looks at you. And your sheep's eyes when you look back. You've got a case on him – much good may it do you. Because you put one foot wrong and I'll horsewhip the both of you!'

Julia responded to the coarse accusation without proper thought. She slapped Ralph's jeering face.

A snarl of disbelieving rage contorted his features. 'You uppity, insubordinate bitch!'

He snatched up a whiskey bottle by its neck and with a sudden swing buried the weighted base of it deep into her soft belly.

The breath rushed out between Julia's lips and she doubled up and fell to the floor, clutching her bruised midriff. She moaned piteously.

Buckhampton ignored his young wife's writhings. He broached the bottle, taking a lip-smacking swig of its fiery contents.

'You need taking in hand, Julia. Strip off and get into that bed. I know what you need. When I've taken care of this bottle, I'm going to take care of you!'

He leered. One pleasure at a time. In due course, he would exercise his right to tame her, bend her to his will.

Julia was filled with revulsion. She went to plead, but found she couldn't. She struggled wordlessly to her feet. Tears of pain and anguish trickled onto her pink cheeks, and fell like a sprinkling of first raindrops onto the smooth-planed and varnished floorboards.

The hubbub and smell of mining and its ancillary operations were continuously in the background in Silver Leaf, but the exertions of the day in the dry, rarefied mountain air had brought Tod Larraby swift and deep sleep on retiring. Nevertheless, he was awake and alert the instant the soft tapping sounded at the door of his room.

His hand went to the Colt under his pillow and he thrust aside the covers. 'Who is it?' he demanded in an even voice neither loud nor soft.

'Julia … Lady Buckhampton,' came the unexpected reply.

Larraby mused, but found no ready answer to the question he asked himself. So he said, 'What do you want – Julia?'

Back came an anxious answer. 'I have to speak to you, Tod.'

'Tonight? Now?'

'Yes, oh *yes.*' Faced with his incredulity,

she was emphatic.

Larraby swore under his breath. He pulled on shirt and denims over his longjohns and padded unbooted to the door.

'What's the trouble?' he asked outright when he'd let her in. 'This isn't in order.' Naturally, he was reflecting seriously over the decency of entertaining a respectable woman – his boss's wife and a titled lady in English society moreover – in such circumstances. He could be making a bad mistake.

She understood he was uneasy, and why. 'Don't worry,' she said. 'My husband – indeed no one – will know I've been here. I read your room number off the book on the desk.'

Larraby ran his fingers through his unruly thatch of brown hair, flecked at the sides with grey. His face was grim and hard as he lighted a lamp.

'Something must be wrong,' he stated flatly, pushing aside his concern at her presence in his room.

'Everything's wrong!' she said.

'How's that?'

'You must persuade my husband to abandon this trip, or I fear it will be the death of us all.'

'It won't be easy an' I don't recommend it for womenfolks, but if it's what his lordship wants…'

'It will be impossible! Ralph will make it so.' She shuddered. 'Do you know what he's doing at this moment?'

'Sleeping?' Larraby ventured.

'Lying in a stupor would be a better description! He's very much the worse for drink, though the better that is for me, or I would have been abused unmercifully.'

Larraby's head came up sharply and his eyes searched Julia's face, finding the red rims and faint puffiness around her eyes. 'He's beaten you, made you cry!' he said with sudden perception.

'He struck me in the stomach with a full bottle of whiskey, but that's not even the half of the problem. He means to take whiskey with him on our trip into the mountains. It can only promote disaster, I know. The whole thing is ill-founded. Ralph has two obsessions – liquor and his precious brat of a son, Lord John.'

Larraby was shaken by Julia's vehemence in denouncing her husband as a tyrannical wifebeater and drunkard. He frowned.

'Forgive my – uh – impertinence, but I don't know's I've been told enough, even as a hired hand,' he said. 'Suppose we start with this Johnny Lord.'

It seemed a good opener to him. He might have insisted on the facts of Buckhampton's relationship with his wife. But the new knowledge of Buckhampton's cruelty had fired up a deep-burning anger inside him. Talking of the vanished son would neither feed its flames so actively, nor aggravate the raw wound of the woman's distress.

'Johnny Lord is the false name adopted by Lord John Sloan in the Americas,' Julia began. 'Lord John had blackened his book badly at home. He has a latent, rakish charm, but more notably he's a vicious n'er-do-well without scruple or honour. There were gambling debts and brawls and wronged women. He deflowered a housemaid who was the daughter of Lord Buckhampton's oldest retainer. Ralph was virtually obliged to send him abroad to escape the wrath of society and the London courts.'

'His father disowned him then?'

'Oh no, you misunderstand. Lord John is withal the apple of his father's eye. At bottom, the boy follows his sire's creed: You have no friends in this life – you take what you want or it's taken from you.'

'It's a code I've come across,' Larraby commented sombrely.

'I'm sure it is, Tod. The Sloans are in good company on the American frontier. I would not be the first Englishwoman to note that "smartness" is all here. Over-reaching your neighbour in every fashion not illegal is the quality held in the greatest repute. The Godlessness would have horrified the Pilgrim Fathers.'

Larraby nodded. 'Good men are sorry it

should be so,' he said. 'Though I don't doubt Johnny Lord found it a nice place to keep on his hell-raising.'

'Precisely. Ralph had an itinerary drawn up for him, visiting the ranches and mines in which he has invested a large part of his fortune.'

'British capital finances much of the cattle industry,' Larraby agreed. 'Railroads the same.'

'You are right. Ralph owns great herds of cattle and vast tracts of land, some acquired through dummy entrymen. But chasing all this up was too tame for Lord John and he abandoned it apparently. He took to what you call the owlhoot trail.'

'And lit out into the wilderness.'

'So everyone reports. His father wants him back...' She sighed wearily. 'You've seen what he's like, Tod. Rude, ruthless, possessive. Intolerant of those who would stand in his way, be it on the path to power and wealth or in the satisfying of a foolish fancy. He'll do anything to get what he wants.'

‘Even beat his wife,’ Larraby said softly.

She lowered her face, as though in shame. ‘Even that.’

Larraby punched a fist into his other, open palm. ‘He’ll not do it again for many a day, by God,’ he said fiercely. ‘Not while we ride the trail together.’

Julia’s alarm quickened again. ‘What’s that? You mean to persevere with this madness, in spite of all I’ve told you?’

‘No way can I leave it alone,’ Larraby told her. ‘I won’t bother your head with the details, but the choice for me is between serving your husband or a spell in a jailhouse cell and maybe the state pen.’

‘Oh…!’ she cried, closing her eyes in despair. ‘I might have known it. Everyone I meet here is a lackey of my beast of a husband. Then the first decent man to come along and not grovel to him bears the brand of a criminal!’

‘No matter,’ Larraby muttered, abashed. ‘It can’t be all bad. Leastways I’ll be on hand to curb Buckhampton’s excesses. But when you get back to England, you must leave him. Divorce him, or whatever.'

An obvious thought struck Larraby so unexpectedly that he put it into words without thinking. 'Beats me how you ever got hitched to such a swine.'

Julia hung her head. 'The marriage was a folly I now deeply regret,' she said contritely. 'I was previously married to a dashing officer in the Guards who was killed in a boating mishap. The tragedy of his death must have stolen my reason. In Ralph I saw security, a title and luxuries I could only dream of on a widow's pension. I soon discovered my error in these fond imaginings.'

'I reckon Buckhampton could never have deserved you.'

'It was my own fault. For being willing to marry someone I didn't love.' She spoke bitterly. 'For aspiring to a congenial life and putting it above all else.'

Larraby knew he could only begin to glimpse the grim realities of her sorry life story. He felt a huge sympathy for her –

trapped in a marriage entered into too quickly and for all the wrong reasons.

The tears were welling up again in Julia's eyes. She had every right to self-pity, he thought. Tentatively, he put an arm around her, intending to comfort her.

'You poor little lady,' he murmured with a simple, honest sincerity.

What happened next took him by complete surprise. He was even a little shocked by the intensity of her reaction.

Julia pulled herself close to him, her cheeks flushed, and kissed him full on his still-parted lips, her mouth working hungrily. It was a second before he responded in kind, feeling the heat of her tongue against his teeth.

It was many more seconds before they broke apart, breathing heavily, looking at one another, eye to eye, for a long and wondering moment. Their hearts pounded.

She swallowed hard, and made a brave bid to explain herself. 'You must think I'm a terrible hussy,' she said in a low voice. 'But

I couldn't help myself. It's been so long since a real man has shown me any true kindness and affection.'

'You mustn't blame yourself,' he said. 'You're in awful distress an' not thinking aright, I guess.'

'No! That isn't everything. I'm so glad I've met you, Tod Larraby. For months I've been keeping myself from my husband and our marriage bed. He reeked of liquor; he was unclean. That withdrawal, though necessary for my sanity, has been dearly bought in other ways.'

'I don't figure, Julia...'

But Larraby was beginning to, sort of, for Julia was a healthy woman in her prime, and her next words confirmed his guess.

'My first husband was in every sense a full man, and deliciously demanding. Like a – a stallion! I'm no paragon of chastity but a grown woman made of ordinary stuff.' Julia's white teeth nibbled nervously at her wobbling lower lip while her eyes glistened with moistness. Larraby wondered what she might dare say next. But he said nothing, and Julia continued. 'I've missed him deeply. Being cruelly used by a self-important man who hasn't cared a fig for my needs has been a poor substitute.'

Larraby said, 'Do you want me to kiss you again?'

'Yes, Tod, yes! I want you to do *everything* to me.'

She flung herself against him, wrapping her arms around his broad shoulders. She moaned as his lips touched hers, and opened her mouth, letting his tongue find hers.

Gently, but with no great effort, he lifted her off her feet and carried her to his bed. Fingers trembling with haste worked at buttons and clasps and buckles. Soon dress and shift, shirt, denims and longjohns were mingled in a discarded heap on the floor.

7

Secret Tracker

Julia had left Tod Larraby's room some hours earlier and the coming dawn was turning the windows of his hotel room grey. He got up and looked out. Hoar-frost sparkled on rails and ledges, but the streets were otherwise gloomy and the air cold. While the sun had not yet risen, the everlasting snow on the highest peaks of the ranges to the west had taken on a rose-red flush. The lower, timbered slopes stayed chill, dark and indigo except where the pines were tipped with the ghostly silver frost.

Later, the same dry day would bring the blazing heat of summer.

Larraby speculated as to how his companions on the pack trip into the mountains would cope with these contrasting extremities. He'd stowed away in his own canvas bedroll a heavy wool jacket to wear in the event of unseasonable storms in the high passes. He'd warned the Buckhamptons to equip themselves similarly.

The expedition could last a matter of a week or drag on for a month, during which time the English couple would be totally out of touch with the civilization they were accustomed to.

If, as Flame had told him, Johnny Lord was holing up with the Jet Konaskis bunch, the kid would not be easily tracked down. Only the outlaws knew just where the notorious Camp was. Rumour said it lay on the meadow of a high, rock-girdled park hidden somewhere among a network of canyons. Tortuous trails ran snake-like through the mountains gashed by these inaccessible ravines, but many led to dead ends. Larraby had seen enough of the country to know it would be difficult to light on the right one to Konaskis' domain.

And if they did, extreme caution would be necessary. No nosey marshal or sheriff had ever seen the Camp and come back to tell about it.

A circumspect approach and an unannounced arrival would be desirable. Jet Konaskis ruled his roost with an iron hand and might look with disfavour upon intruders of their kind.

They also said Konaskis liked to kill – with bare hands or gun – and was fast and good with either.

Larraby turned back to the room and took in the rumpled state of his bedsheets and blankets. The scent of lovers' pleasure clung in the closed air; salty, almost metallic. His heart seemed to sink into his stomach. The thought of taking a woman on this perilous expedition had been bad enough, but now it seemed doubly worse.

Their lovemaking of the night just past had been enthusiastic and satisfying. They'd neither had misgivings, and afterwards there'd been no regrets. But now Larraby felt a deep remorse.

The encounter had added fresh complications to an adventure that already had the smell of disaster. He had made a mistake in getting involved with Julia. Being constantly in her company yet keeping up a sham of indifference to her in front of the bullying Lord Buckhampton would be far from easy.

And could he trust Julia to keep their liaison secret, let alone not aggravate the tensions already between himself and Buckhampton?

The conclusion that he'd made a fool of himself over a woman was a heavy worry on his mind. It was something he'd not done since before the War, when he'd been a shave-a-week youth. There'd been other women, sure, but Julia was something very different. What scared him most was that she'd wanted him as much as he had her.

He had no illusions that a man like himself could occupy a lasting place in her life. Not only was she a married woman, but their backgrounds were so hugely diverse.

‘The pure truth of it is you should’ve showed her your door,’ Larraby told himself. But he was glad he hadn’t.

From doorways and under awnings and along the boardwalks, the idlers and the men and few women who went about their business in Silver Leaf paused to watch the string that rode out from the livery stable and proceeded up the wide strip of Main Street.

Lord Buckhampton took the lead on a black stallion, a wiry, muscular animal with the lines of a mustang. Behind him rode his wife on a sorrel pony, and Larraby brought up the rear on his own saddle mount, straightening out the three pack horses into a tidy line.

Buckhampton’s black pranced along, eager to be moving, and needed restraining, but the pack animals were content to lag. They were older and wiser in the ways of such journeyings and took up a plodding gait they could hold to through the long trip ahead.

Julia was kitted out in a thick, half-fitting jacket, a skirt reaching to the ankles and full-cut trousers gathered into frills which fell over the tops of her boots. Thus modesty was preserved when she swung into her pony's conventional saddle. Under Buckhampton's baleful glare, nobody showed the least sign of shock, but all were as respectful as could be.

Larraby thought Julia's costume both serviceable and feminine, though he held his tongue and made no comment.

Among the watchers observing their departure was the dusky-skinned, sultry-eyed Flame. In search of darning thread at a haberdasher's, the startling attraction from Madame Levanne's had made one of her rare excursions across the invisible line in the dust that marked off the red-light district of Lower Cross Street from the respectable parts of town.

Frowningly, she recognized Tod Larraby as the stranger who'd gratified her in availing himself of her services and whom she'd told about her reckless beau.

Flame was unable to contain her curiosity. A niggle of what might also be alarm teased her world-wise brain.

The ageing hostler at the livery stable shoved his chewing tobacco into one leathery cheek and swallowed heavily when she approached him. His Adam's apple bobbed and his complexion darkened.

'Tain't none o' yore business who they is or where they's goin',' he told her discouragingly.

The hostler was no more than a menial frontier roustabout but a man had his pride. Soiled doves had no right to question a man so. Red blood still flowed in his veins. He appreciated the statuesque figure of the girl, with its full breasts, slim waist, curving hips and long legs. Her smooth, warm-coloured skin made a feller's fingers itch to touch. But he had to keep a mind for his reputation.

Flame's dark eyes smouldered. 'You tell me what I ask, or I'll walk right on into your harness room and unlace my bodice. Then I will rake your face with my fingernails and scream.'

The hostler gulped and almost lost his cud down his scrawny throat.

'Why, you mongrel bitch!' he jerked out.

'Careful, white rat!' Flame hissed. 'For I am very serious.'

The man hesitated tremblingly and his eyes went out on stalks as her long, supple fingers toyed at her collar.

'Yuh're crazy, but I'll tell yuh an' it won't do yuh no good nohow!' he gasped, mentally squirming. 'Them folks gotta lot more guts than brains. Takes a blind idjut to ride into outlaw country, an' thet's where they's goin' – lookin' fer a bucko called Johnny Lord.'

Murder blazed in Flame's eyes. 'Is that so?'

'Thet's what I said,' the hostler said truculently.

Now it was Flame who was discomposed, but she followed a profession that had taught her well how to mask her true feelings.

'Who are they?' she demanded curtly.

The stable hand sneered. 'High-toners – way out o' yore class. Lord Buckhampton an' his fancy dame all the way from England.'

The name Buckhampton meant nothing to Flame, but she knew her Johnny was from England and that he had kicked over the traces there, too, before coming to America. He'd told her as much, bragging of the women he had compromised there, the jealousy and wrath of husbands and fathers; and of the illegal games of chance and prizefighting by which he'd stolen other men's fortunes.

'I'm a terrible rotter, y'know,' Johnny would say waggishly, when making some particularly disgraceful demand of her. 'Not a spark of decency in me!'

She had never seen her Johnny do a real day's work in his life. Maybe that was part of his attraction for her. But were his confessed foolishnesses catching up with him? It occurred to Flame that the English couple might well be angry pursuers from Johnny's past, seeking retribution.

'But the other man,' she asked aloud, 'what of him?'

'A saddle bum,' the hostler growled. 'Reck'n he's the biggest fool of all. The kind who kin put up a good fight with a gun, I guess, but he ain't no big-shot outlaw like Jet Konaskis.'

'Why is he with the English? Is he a lawman in disguise?' Flame voiced her wildest imagining – that her erstwhile client was an undercover federal marshal to whom she'd betrayed her roguish lover.

'How would I know?' the old man said. In his own mind, he'd tagged Larraby as a hombre operating on the other side of the law, but he sensed Flame's agitation and felt vindictive enough to exacerbate it. 'Hell, *I* don't pry into no other folks' affairs. Oh, no, not me!'

'But you've spoken with him?'

'I warned him when he came inta town them mountains ain't healthy, but my opinion ain't important, y'see, an' he's fixed hisself up as the Buckhamptons' guide. Or thet's how the tale's told.'

The hostler grinned at her mockingly, not at all sure how he'd gotten the upper hand in this bizarre interview, but enjoying it just the same.

The half-breed gnawed at her lower lip in an agony of uncertainty. Then she seemed abruptly to come to a decision.

'All right, little man,' she said. 'I'll have to find out for myself.'

She turned on her high heels and left the barn in a purposeful hurry.

The trail out of Silver Leaf pushed through country that bore the scars of mining on every side. Charred stumps dotted hillside ledges where the pines had been felled wholesale to clear the way for man's frenzied excavations.

'It's like some dreadful blight,' Julia said to Larraby. 'There's hardly a green thing to be seen.'

Narrow, switchback foot trails ascended steep heights to black holes in the rock face that were the timber-shored portals to prospectors' tunnels.

Digging, blasting, burrowing … here men had sought the treasure they thought would bring them happiness and ease. To some it had brought only a plot in the cemetery on Silver Leaf's boundary.

'Mining turns the earth inside out,' Julia went on. 'It destroys nature and, I fear, many hearts, too.'

Her husband scoffed. 'Pshaw! Larraby doesn't want to hear your soft women's talk, my dear. Mining creates prosperity – railroads, towns, cities, where ambitious men can grow and thrive. So we'll have an end to this whining!'

Julia fell silent. But Larraby couldn't help keep watching her – back straight, legs faintly bent at the knees, her weight perfectly distributed upon the horse's back. Buckhampton was at least right about one thing: she was clearly a person born to the saddle.

By noon they were clear of the devastated landscape, striking upwards on a difficult ascent through the green gloom of pitch-pine thickets and through narrow passes carved out over countless centuries by the narrow streams that had beds in their depths. Sometimes fantastic formations of bright red rock overhung the trail. Crested blue-jays scolded at their passing.

Once or twice a prickling of the short hairs at his neck gave Larraby the eerie sensation that other eyes observed them, too, but he put it down to nerves. On one occasion Larraby thought he glimpsed through a clump of pines a mounted figure wearing fringed buckskin.

'There!' he yelled, pointing to the rim of the broken heights they were skirting.

'What is it, man?' Buckhampton rapped, reining in his mettlesome horse.

'Somebody foll'ring us. I saw the rider skylined just then.'

Buckhampton peered up through the needled boughs and saw nothing. 'There's nobody,' he said blisteringly. 'Let's stop dragging our heels.'

'Hang it!' Larraby muttered. 'He must've drawn back.'

Buckhampton was scathing. 'Or you're dreaming, Larraby.'

During the morning they also met on the road several prospectors and a couple of elk hunters, but in the afternoon their route took them above the timber-line into unfrequented and desolate uplands. Here the footing for the horses was often bad, across expanses of large and small boulders like Larraby had heard called lava beds.

'Circumstances don't admit of making a fuss,' Julia said quietly to Larraby, 'but will the way be all so barren?'

'No, ma'am,' Larraby said subserviently. He was strongly aware that Buckhampton strained his ears to listen in on every word that passed between them. 'There are fine mountain pastures hidden in the ranges. They call 'em parks.'

'Parks?'

Larraby was well enough read to know what images the word might conjure to a woman used to an English lord's estates. Trim lawns, shrubbery and lichened brick walls, lodges, mansions, squirrels and deer maybe, forelock-tugging gamekeepers.

He gave her the lowdown on parks, Colorado style.

'The biggest is South Park. It's a great rolling prairie 70 miles long and 10,000 feet high. In winter it'd be near closed by snow, but it's well-grassed and watered, with flowery meadows blue and yellow in summer. Game makes it a paradise for hunters.'

'Will we find Lord John in one of these parks?'

Larraby didn't want to alarm Julia by mentioning ruffianly outlaw bands, but he knew Konaskis' hideout was reputed to lie in a high, pleasant valley girded completely by snow-capped mountains rising to 15,000 feet, their rugged slopes irregularly grown with pine forests and gouged by deep canyons, wooded and boulder-strewn.

‘Who knows?’ he said with a shrug. ‘There’s hundreds of parks large and small scattered through the Rockies, most of ’em still empty and unnamed.’

Buckhampton had grown impatient with their chat. The trail twisted off the lava-bed plateau and plunged down into a timbered gorge. It narrowed onto a ledge and the footing was still precarious, all loose stones and flints. But the testy Englishman took the tricky descent at a rush. He gave the highly-strung black its head and sent showers of the natural debris underhoof clattering off the steep edge into the abyss below.

Larraby shook his head in reproof. ‘Bull-headed galoot. I thought I was s’pposed to lead the show.’

Even Larraby didn’t foresee how calamitous the results were going to be.

8

Death Plunge

Though the trail was barely wide enough for two horses, Larraby nudged his bay up alongside Julia. When they were stirrup to stirrup, he leaned across and put out a strong hand to grasp the bridle of the woman's even-tempered sorrel.

'Better let him make it first. Ain't no sense in piling on top of him if he tumbles.'

Her face pale, Julia nodded. They watched with drawn breath as Lord Buckhampton's horse slithered down the dangerous grade in a cloud of dust and grit.

A stand of stunted pines with an undergrowth of dwarf spruce and brambles bordered the trail where it eventually opened out. The precipitate and noisy arrival of man and horse within a hundred yards of the point startled a nursing she-bear, which lumbered from the trees into Buckhampton's road.

The grizzly, dark brown with a 'collar' of lighter hair, was a full-grown specimen, probably about five years old. And she felt that she, and her three cubs secreted in the brush, were threatened.

She roared her disapproval.

The excitable black stallion panicked. Nostrils distended in a wild snort, he reared up, front hoofs climbing air.

The alerted cubs lolloped from the brush and fled in different directions. Denied the chance to retreat in good order, the female grizzly appeared confused.

Larraby shouted to Buckhampton to pull back. Bear attacks on men were rare unless the hairy beasts were cornered, injured or provoked by dogs. But an irritable, weaning she-bear's reactions defied the rules. Anxiety could readily turn to aggression.

This one extended her head and neck and

laid back her ears. She rotated, stepping first one way, then the other. Finally, she wheeled and attacked, swatting out with her mighty forepaws.

Buckhampton was unable to control his frantic horse, which pranced and plunged and squealed in terror.

'Hot damn!' Larraby roared. 'You better quit it fast, sir!'

But Buckhampton had already lost control of the situation. The bucking black threw him out of the saddle and bolted back up the trail.

Larraby pulled in front of Julia's pony just in time to let the spooked black storm past without crashing into them. In places, the trail was the frightening width of a goat-track, and the drop to one side was dizzying to look over. As the stallion brushed past, foam from its mouth and flecks of lather spattered them. The stench of the horse's sweated fear made their own mounts fidget nervously.

Behind them, the laden pack animals

didn't fare as well. Buckhampton's hurtling horse slammed into the first of them, shoulder to shoulder with a sickening thud and a shrill whinnying.

There was a scrabbling of hoofs on the loose rock, then a scream as the hit pack horse stumbled and fell forward onto its knees. Almost in slow motion it went over the edge of the track and crashed horrifyingly down the near-vertical slope, starting a miniature avalanche and scattering its load in bouncing fragments.

The doomed animal somersaulted through the air and plummeted head-first on the last stage of its drop onto the rocks at a stream edge many hundreds of feet below. It landed with a meaty thump that resounded through the gorge and its broken body lay unmoving.

All this Larraby could witness only helplessly out of the corner of his eye. His prime concern was in front of him, where his unsaddled employer stood face to face with an enraged grizzly.

Larraby had never fought a bear before

and he was damn sure Buckhampton hadn't. But he'd met frontiersmen who had and he'd heard the stories and seen the ugly scars on scalps, arms, legs and torsos.

The bear would knock her opponent down with murderous rips of paws equipped with curved claws four inches long, or simply bowl him over with sheer weight and momentum. She would move in, biting repeatedly, and crush the bloody victim in a furry death hug.

Larraby's hand hovered for a moment over the stock of the repeating rifle carried in his saddle scabbard. But he debated against unstowing it. Though most effective in fire power, the Winchester's advantages were at longer range than this, and the shifting dance of man and bear could well see the wrong one receiving his lead.

He dropped to the ground and handed up the bay's reins to Julia. He also drew his .44 revolver.

'Here – hold the horses! This looks rough. His lordship's got the critter plenty riled.'

Buckhampton had been badly winded by

his bruising tumble from the back of his horse. But he'd been back on his feet fast, and was backing off up the trail, so far keeping out of range of the lumbering bear whose eye was partly distracted by keeping tabs on her scattered litter.

The two men met – and Buckhampton promptly seized Larraby by the left arm and propelled him forward.

'Earn your goddamn hire!' he ordered. 'Shoot the beast!'

Larraby stumbled forward on the unstable dirt and almost lost his balance.

'Tod!' Julia screamed from behind him in warning.

Almost at once, she recognized the inappropriateness of addressing Larraby so familiarly. She put her wrist to her mouth and bit at her cuff as though she could still muffle the unwise use of his first name.

But Buckhampton seemed not to notice. Then, as soon as he reached the point where his wife waited, he was busy getting his left, French-calfskin boot into the stirrup of Larraby's bay, made skittery by his brutal haste.

'Stand still, crowbait!' he snarled. His one interest was to get himself into a saddle fast so he could hightail it if that became necessary.

Larraby was by a miracle still on his feet. But the bear was close enough to take a swat at him with a huge paw. If not for his hat's crown, his scalp would have been laid open by the ripping claws. As it was, two nasty scratches dampened the hair at his right temple with blood.

The drawn Colt kicked twice in Larraby's fist, spitting flame and lead. The heavy roar of the exploding shells battered against eardrums.

The bear grunted in aggravation – and kept on coming.

Larraby never loaded all six chambers of his revolver. For reasons of safety, he left the hammer resting on an empty one. That meant without reloading he had three more chances to stop the bear – one more than had already proved ineffective.

The third shot hit the bear in the throat.

A dark round hole showed against the lighter band of hair at the neck. At such close range it punched right through fur and tissue, making a wider and uglier wound at its point of exit. Blood spurted in a crimson fountain, sprinkling Larraby, though his face was already streaked with his own.

And the bear kept on coming!

Desperately, Larraby emptied his six-shooter into the menacing, shambling bulk looming over him. He dodged another swing of the scimitar-like claws, but his riding boots weren't made for fancy footwork and he tripped and went over sideways.

That probably saved his life.

Julia cried out a second time as the she-bear finally fell. Four hundred and fifty pounds of solid flesh and bone crashed to the ground, partly across Larraby's legs.

The bear was down – kicking, squirming, dying.

Larraby freed himself. He was bruised and shaken, but not badly hurt. Swiftly, he thumbed open the Colt's loading gate and ejected the spent shells, sending them rattling to the stony ground around his feet. With trembling fingers, he filled several chambers, and pushed the loading gate back into place. Then he bent over the jerking bear and put a slug through her brain.

The one shot terminated the creature's death agonies.

Retrieving his clawed hat, Larraby beat the dust from his trousers and started back to rejoin the Buckhamptons.

'Now, Larraby,' said the man, dismounting, 'you're running this show for me. Catch me the black and we'll make tracks.'

From behind his back, Julie looked down at Larraby with a despairing look. Her thoughts were easy to read; she was glad Larraby was safe, but after his clash with the bear, a moment for him to catch his breath would not be unreasonable.

She said tentatively, 'Ralph, perhaps you or I could–'

'Hold your tongue, Julia!' Buckhampton

snarled. 'Larraby's contracted to do it. My business is to give the orders.'

Larraby touched his head, assuring himself that although a lot of his blood was about, his wound was not serious. He gave Buckhampton no verbal answer, but strode off toward the stallion, swabbing his blood-stained brow with his neckerchief.

The horse stood facing him, trembling all over. Larraby reached for the trailing reins.

'Now cut it out, you ornery critter,' he said … whereupon the baulky animal tossed its mane, turned around, threw up his heels several times, and went plunging off in the direction of the lava beds. The cinch had come loose and Buckhampton's slipped saddle blanket was left behind.

Larraby returned to the others and climbed into the familiar saddle of his bay to set off in pursuit.

The black was off the trail, galloping in erratic circles through a jumble of rocks and boulders – centuries-old debris deposited by forces long quiescent. Buckhampton's saddle was now over his shoulders and the stirrups bouncing against his sides.

Larraby spurred the surefooted bay into a canter. As he rode, he unhitched the rope that hung at his saddle. He was no top hand with a lasso, but he was handy, and the coils of untanned hide were supple and free of kinks.

Speed and surprise were on Larraby's side. When he was almost alongside the black, the pursued horse wheeled, trapped by the littered rocks in an enclosed space. Larraby's rope snaked through the air. Momentarily, the noose seemed to hang in the air above the black's head before it fell over his head, and Larraby pulled up hard, setting the bay back almost on to his haunches.

Larraby was pleased to have the chase over. 'Got you, my friend! An' I don't figure to let you go!'

But he knew getting the better of a runaway black horse was far from the finish of his problems. He led the horse back to where the

Buckhamptons waited with the surviving pack animals and hobbled him, though he'd already quieted down considerably.

Larraby looked over the edge of the chasm.

The dead horse and its wide-flung load looked inaccessible to any but practised and equipped mountaineers.

'Seen enough?' Buckhampton asked sarcastically.

'That was the tents we lost,' Larraby told him. 'One I can't even see. Reckon it must've been swept off downstream, which leaves us about all washed up.'

'How do you make that out?' Buckhampton asked.

Larraby stayed mild despite the earl's terseness. 'We'll have to go back to Silver Leaf to replace them. We could make it by late evening if we don't dawdle.'

'Bugger that!' the Englishman retorted vulgarly. 'Listen, my fellow, I'm not about to waste a whole day's riding. We go on without the goddamned tents if need be!'

Larraby drew the line at an attempt to retrieve them. The descent was a perilous feat of mountaineering he was not game to tackle. The ribs of solid rock were smooth granite, offering little by way of handholds or footholds. The broken stuff looked loose enough to give way and tumble as soon as touched.

He shrugged. 'Ain't no horse-sense in busting my neck trying to get them back, that's certain sure,' he muttered dourly. 'So it's no tents, I guess.'

He turned to Julia. 'I'm sorry about that, ma'am.'

'She sighed expressively. 'It was none of your fault – Mr Larraby.'

Her husband seized on the split-second hesitation before her deliberate forming of their guide's name. It reminded him that in the extremity of the alarm over the bear, she'd called him Tod.

'*Mr* Larraby,' he sneered. 'So you remember yourself now, do you, my dear wife?'

'H-how do you mean?'

Buckhampton laughed. The fact that except for comment on the landscape Larraby and Julia had exchanged few words during the day meant nothing. In fact, it merely served to strengthen his suspicion that some sort of absurd attraction had sprung up between them.

He'd told Julia before how he'd seen her eyes follow Larraby like a lovesick girl. And she was still doing it. She couldn't help herself. He knew women. He saw the signs. She was smitten with the desperado.

Buckhampton burned inwardly with a mounting, jealous rage. Larraby was tall and broad-shouldered and of many fewer years than himself. Walking or riding his hard, muscled body moved with a certain fluid grace. That all too easily might appeal to someone of an impressionable and sentimental disposition... Like his still-young wife who unhealthily deprived her physical self by employing every excuse to keep him from her bed.

Buckhampton didn't let the matter rest

with his ugly laugh. He said tauntingly, 'You look a trifle pale, Julia.'

'A want of sleep, I expect.'

Buckhampton glowered. 'Just be warned – the pair of you – that you can't make a cuckold of me. Try it and I'll take payment in full!'

9

The Earl Uses His Fists

Flame rode a pony less than fourteen hands high. Johnny Lord had bought it for her from a mountain man who said it had been bred by his allies, the Ute Indians. With its patterned coat she suspected it might have some Appaloosa blood and that it, or its sire or dam, might in fact have been stolen.

Whatever its history, it was at home in the mountains and went places that might have daunted a goat without a flicker. Its colouring gave it natural camouflage, an advantage Flame was appreciating as she picked her way along rocky shelves and through the shadowed greenness of timber, stalking the tracks of the English couple and their gunfighter guide.

For Flame was now certain in her suspicious mind that gunfighter was the calling of the capable client who'd called on her at Madame Levanne's. She'd seen his Colt .44 with the catch filed down for hair-trigger quickness in pumping out every bullet in its chambers. Why hadn't she thought of that before?

Perhaps she had and at the time it hadn't mattered.

'He has gunfighter written all over him,' she murmured, her head filling with malice.

Gunfighters came in two varieties. There were the outlaws, like Clay Allison, John Wesley Hardin and Jesse James. And there were the lawmen, like the Earp brothers, Bat Masterson and Wild Bill Hickock.

It made no difference to a woman when she was selling her body. But if this one was on the trail of her beloved Johnny Lord, she could think only in terms of pursuit and the administering of so-called justice, which to her mind was another name for the settling of scores.

She remembered how Larraby had questioned her – persistently it now seemed – and how she'd told him Johnny was headed for the Camp of Jet Konaskis. *Betrayed* Johnny, she thought, deeply ruing her loose tongue. Because she surely feared Larraby and the high-faluting English folks were no ordinary tourist party.

Such people roamed in style, taking in the better-known sights, sampling 'camp cures' and meeting suitably tamed frontier celebrities and Indian chiefs. For the genuine society travellers, there would be spring carriages with camp servants and a string of well-stocked commissary wagons. Iced champagne at sunset...

And their knowledgeable guides kept well away from hostile wilderness.

Elatedly, Flame witnessed the clash with the bear from behind a high crag, her buckskin-clad form flattened against the rocks and her pony obediently ground-hitched well back.

'Bah!' she exclaimed in disgust when the

bear was killed and the panicked stallion rounded up.

She was not especially vindictive, but she did exult when high-and-mighty white folks got their comeuppance. Maybe it was a hangover from her earlier days when mixed parentage had made her too often the victim of other children's cruel slurs and practical jokes. Only with the coming of adulthood had the persecution ceased, though she suspected deep down that she was still despised, even by the men who used her.

Unseen, she slithered back Indian-fashion to her pony through brush that didn't look as though it would hide a good-sized jack rabbit let alone a generously endowed woman.

The man who looked like a gunfighter – lawman or outlaw – was very smart and brave, but he'd fooled her, and his expedition had to be stopped from finding Johnny before she could get to him first and warn him.

'It's not such a tall order,' she told herself.

'Come dark, I'll find a way to settle their hash!'

Larraby struck an old Indian trail into the mountains, but the party came across no sign of recent human habitation. The outlaws' hideout was going to be plenty difficult to locate, and as the sun sank Larraby wondered if Lord Buckhampton would be so confident about the quest if he'd known how imprecisely he was planning their wanderings. His best hope of finding the place lay in a chance meeting-up with some of the sweepings of the West who resided there.

The Camp was notorious the length and breadth of the mining country. It was a known refuge and base for thieves, murderers and renegades of every stripe. Konaskis' bunch and its hangers-on had to make their comings and goings sometime, some way.

Sunset was magnificent. Colour rioted in the sky and the white peaks became crimson and gold.

They cached the horses in a rock-rimmed

hollow, rich in fine, sun-cured hay which, as Larraby pointed out, would enable them to conserve their supplies of grain feed.

A sombre cluster of pines was reflected with the golden sky in the clear depths of a small lake where it was not covered by the white blooms and dark green pads of lilies.

'There's water and plenty of dry wood close,' Larraby said. 'A good spot to pitch camp.'

'Roll up in our blankets, you mean,' corrected Julia, and quickly returned to silence at a dirty look from her husband.

Larraby had other ideas. 'I know enough wood lore to throw up a brush leanto, sir. It will give you an' your wife some privacy and shelter from the frost.'

While Larraby set to, arranging pine limbs for framework, Buckhampton sat by and drank the best part of a bottle of whiskey.

Julia began unstrapping pots and pans from a pack saddle, neatly laying them out on a piece of tarpaulin. From the tight line of her jaw, Larraby knew she was fuming at

Buckhampton's inactivity. For God's sake, could he not even stoop to gathering some wood for a small cookfire?

When Larraby had completed the rough shelter to his satisfaction, he started to gather the firewood himself, but Julia stayed him.

'No. I insist you stop now and kindly allow me to clean up the blood on your wounded head.'

Larraby saw she was determined and that Buckhampton had reached a state of partial drowsiness. 'I'll fetch some water,' he said quietly.

'I proposed to use whiskey for the task, to prevent any infection,' Julia said. 'My husband has brought more than enough along, and I can't imagine that any of it will be put to better use.'

She appropriated a bottle from Buckhampton's carpet-bag and uncapped it. A tingle of admiration for her rebellious spirit ran through Larraby.

Buckhampton laughed bleakly when he

saw what was going on but didn't stir himself to intervene. 'Buttering up the scoundrel,' he told no one in particular, his eyes focused on the label of the bottle he was holding.

The spirit stung the raw scratches. Larraby gasped, and Julia winced. 'It looks most fierce,' she said, but persisted till the caked blood was removed and the edges of the torn skin looked clean and pink. She finished by binding his head with a strip torn from a spare petticoat.

'Thank you,' he said gruffly, his eyes still smarting.

Afterward, together, they coaxed a small fire into flame in a rough hearth fashioned from four rocks placed to funnel the cold breeze from the mountains into a steady draught.

They were dog-tired but hungry, too. They broiled thick and juicy steaks, and boiled beans and brewed coffee. Larraby also suggested they should eat some of the bread, because in another day it would be stale and hard.

Even Lord Buckhampton did not argue, but tucked in morosely, belching constantly as the food mingled with the whiskey in his complaining gut.

Larraby heated water in the biggest iron pot while they ate and the dishes were soon cleaned.

Despite its tantalizing odour, Buckhampton had scorned the strong black coffee and now he opened a second bottle of whiskey.

'Don't you think you've drunk enough?' Julia entreated in what Larraby thought was a reasonable tone, all considered.

But Buckhampton had progressed to a new stage of belligerence in his cups. 'And who would stop me, woman?' he flared. 'You speak out of turn with your snivelling admonishments! By God! I'm my own master and yours, and I'll do as I like.'

'Of course,' Julia said coldly.

He hiccuped. 'A man like me doesn't have to beg and pray for permission to take a drop of drink!'

'It's been a great deal more than a drop,'

Julia argued.

'Damn you, woman – you'll not count my sips!'

Her chin came up a little. 'Perhaps a spouse has duties you've overlooked.'

'Enough! Get away into that shelter and into your blankets. I'll take this matter up later – *privately.*'

But Julia's disgust had reached a new depth, and maybe Tod Larraby's presence – and the memory of his considerate love-making – gave her new courage.

'I refuse to share the shelter with you in your intoxicated condition,' she declared impassively. 'I'm prepared to sleep under the stars, like Mr Larraby, and breathe unsullied air.'

The bristling earl reddened with rage. Although his young wife's needling criticisms irked him, she was still his property – his chattel, his possession – to use how and when he saw fit. He had not drunk so much that he was unmindful of that.

'Is that a fact now?' he slurred with spiteful venom. 'And maybe you lust to share his bug-ridden bedroll like a common slut!'

Larraby surprised himself by holding his temper. Shorn of its offensive language, however, Buckhampton's accusation was uncomfortably close to the truth. Yet Larraby couldn't feel guilty that he'd accepted Julia when she'd come seeking the comfort of his arms.

He said tonelessly, 'You're out of line, Buckhampton, an' I'd be obliged if you'd keep me out of your ravings.'

Buckhampton didn't take the hint. He swung his glassy-eyed gaze and stared at Larraby in sheer hate. Watching, Julia felt the sudden conviction that her husband had just about forgotten his argument was with her. The enmity between the two men was profound and had always been only inches beneath the surface.

'Huh! I can read your brand plain as paint,' Buckhampton grated. 'You've been making eyes at my wife all day – skirt-chasing, mealy-mouthed bastard!'

Then he threw his bottle at Larraby's head and ran at him, fists swinging.

Larraby just managed to duck the bottle, but the first of Buckhampton's punches glanced off his cheekbone and the second lammed into his hard-muscled midriff. Both blows hurt. Despite his titled background, there was nothing effete about the Englishman. He was solidly built and he had the right amount of liquor aboard to make him insensitive to minor pain.

It was the whiskey that was the wild card here, Larraby thought. Otherwise the odds had to be on his side. He was younger, fitter and faster. And he'd been in rough houses by the score.

He cut off Buckhampton's grunts of satisfaction with his own blow to the body. Stinking of whiskey, the breath whistled out of the aggressor. But Buckhampton gave no ground. His method of fighting was to charge in like a mad old bull, using his weight and his black fury to drive his punches.

Larraby stood up to him, toe to toe,

slugging it out, giving better than he got. Even so, he took some crashing thumps, high and low, that rocked him on his heels. He'd had a hard day of it before this, and his reactions were not all that they should have been. His head was still plenty sore and his legs badly bruised and stiff from the clash with the bear. He felt far from nimble.

While they fought, the golden afterglow of dusk faded and a big half-moon rose, shining starkly through the needled foliage of the pines.

Buckhampton landed a punch in Larraby's left side that could have stoved in a less-powerfully built man's ribs. He also got him in the face again, splitting the inside of his cheek against his teeth.

The taste of his blood refuelled Larraby's determination to teach this wife-molesting bully a needed lesson. But Buckhampton was nowhere near drunk any more. Larraby's jolting punches and an instinctive sensing of danger purged the whiskey fumes from his brain.

He was getting smarter. Buckhampton was a man of strength, yet his ponderous frame was no match for Larraby's iron muscles and rugged fitness, and he knew it. By keeping in close, he robbed Larraby of the chance of hitting him with anything more than short, stabbing punches.

He also had an innate viciousness with which to take advantage of an opponent whose natural inclination was to fight clean.

He butted with his massive head and jolted his knees into Larraby's groin at every opportunity. It was after one such dirty play that he surprised Larraby by sidestepping, then twisting behind him.

Larraby felt a thick arm wrap itself across his chest, pinning his right arm to his ribs down to the elbow. Simultaneously, Buckhampton thrust his other arm under Larraby's left armpit and rammed his stubby thumb under the Westerner's chin.

Larraby flailed uselessly with his free left arm, but Buckhampton had him in a neck-breaking hold, wrenching back his head, so he could see only the star-flecked blackness of the sky and roaring red mist that was his own blood.

Far off – a million miles away, it seemed – he could hear Julia's voice raised in a pleading cry.

'*Stop it!* Oh, please stop it, the pair of you!'

It gave Larraby a bizarre flashback to his boyhood in Missouri when his mother had uttered about the same words when breaking up a backyard scrap he'd had with his older brother.

That had been a punishing tussle, ending in blackened eyes, bloodied noses and no clear victor.

But this, if Buckhampton had his brutish way, was going to be a fight to the death.

10

Flame's Opportunity

The murmur of voices and the alien aromas of coffee and food carried to Flame on the pine-scented breeze of the approaching night. The half-breed woman dismounted, left her pony tied among the trees and went forward cat-footed.

She scouted right round the Buckhamptons' camp, mostly on hands and knees, taking a special interest in the putting-up of the three saddle mounts and two pack horses. A hazy plan was forming in her mind, but she didn't see how she could act on it until the three campers had settled for the night. And then it wouldn't be easy if one of them – say, the gunfighter – was to stand night guard or sleep lightly, alert for disturbance.

She fingered the antler hilt of a nine-inch long bowie knife in a sheath at her belt and let out a stifled sigh. The moon was rising and perhaps it would be a better scheme to ride on through the night and get to the hideout of Jet Konaskis ahead of these two tenderfoot fools and their devious guide.

But this latter course seemed unattractive to her. Pride told her it would be humiliating to run from such pathetic enemies. And Johnny, surely, would expect her to behave more resourcefully.

Then, after a brief exchange of angry words, the two men began fighting.

Flame's heart throbbed with suppressed excitement. Among the many hard lessons life had taught her was that Lady Luck played her frivolous tricks at the most unexpected times, and that the breaks could be good as well as bad. It could pay to cling to her petticoats.

To her sardonic amusement, the fisticuffs shaped up into vicious, all-out combat. The slapping crack of fists against flesh and bone, the grunts and the heavy breathing of the protagonists were sounds that stood out ignobly against the hoot of owls and the distant howling of wolves.

The fine Englishwoman was totally engrossed in the men's struggles, her pretty face screwed up with anguish as she implored them to desist.

Flame could hope for no better cover than this to make a fleeting dash to the hollow where they'd stashed their horses. She made a stooping run, from tree to tree, from rock to rock.

She went quietly. Her moccasin-clad feet made hardly a sound and her footfalls were muffled by the thick grass the moment she reached the hollow. She was also hidden by the rock rim.

She listened, her chest heaving. There was no hint of pursuit, only the grim thuds of the men's fists, the clump and scrape of their boots and the cries of the distraught woman.

Flame picked her way over to where the

horses loomed in the gathering darkness. One of the animals lifted its long head and began a nicker of greeting. Swiftly, she shot out a hand to cover the horse's muzzle. 'Shhh!' she soothed.

Every one of the horses had been hobbled to deter straying during the night. Larraby had taken a two-foot length of rope to each, looped it around one fore fetlock, given it three twists, and tied the two ends about the other fetlock. Hence any movement by a horse had to be at a creeping pace, or by dint of hopping forward, the forefeet raised awkwardly together.

Flame drew her knife and went about her work.

Larraby felt himself blacking out and thought he heard a clicking in his vertebrae. Unless he broke free of Lord Buckhampton's fiendish lock, he would be a goner.

He wondered if the Englishman knew what he was doing – killing the man who was his guide and the only guarantor, of sorts, of his and his wife's safety in this potentially savage land. Buckhampton was well-soaked in tanglefoot, but it had not affected his unexpected skills as a ruthless fighter. Paradoxically, it had maybe sharpened them. If the man was blind to consequences, it was through the medium of his frighteningly foul temper.

Summoning all the strength he had left, Larraby lifted his left foot and thrust back. His high boot heel contacted Buckhampton's shin and he let it slide down to the man's instep before twisting and grinding for all he was worth.

Buckhampton screamed out in fury and not a little agony. His hold slackened a mite. In that instant, Larraby made another supreme effort. He tore himself free, ripping his shirt as he spun around, and smashed his left fist into Buckhampton's jaw, splitting the knuckles. It was like hitting rock.

Buckhampton spat blood and staggered back, but kept on his feet.

Larraby knew he couldn't dare let up till

his opponent was out cold. He went after him, head down, fists going like pistons into the man's thick body in an effort to wind him totally and end the clash that way.

Buckhampton back-pedalled but stuck up stiff thumbs, trying for Larraby's eyes.

Larraby rolled his head away, a manoeuvre which effectively terminated the drumming tattoo he was beating into Buckhampton's solar plexus.

He was out of immediate danger now and Buckhampton was swaying drunkenly from his punches, even as he should have done from the whiskey he'd consumed.

Buckhampton played one last trick. Among the pine limbs Larraby had collected to construct a frame for the brush leanto had been a piece he'd discarded as too thick and too unwieldy. Buckhampton made a fake fallback, stooped and swept it up by the end in both hands.

As Larraby surged forward to press home his onslaught, Buckhampton swung the heavy timber at his head.

Larraby dodged to one side, and the bough that might have cracked his skull like an eggshell whistled past him, missing by a fraction of an inch.

Its unchecked free end went thumping into the ground, its momentum carrying Buckhampton with it. Buckhampton had put all his crazed might into the swing and his grip was now loose. The timber's jarring stop jerked it out of his hands and he tottered, then stumbled to hands and knees.

Larraby was lightning-quick. For the first time Buckhampton was momentarily defenceless – and, battered and sore, Larraby wasn't letting that opening go by. He grabbed up the piece of pine himself and took his own swing with it.

Buckhampton was caught on the shoulder and the side of the head. The swipe hurled him face down into the dirt with such force that a big cloud of dust rose in the pale gleam of the moonshine.

Larry knew with sick relief that the fight was over. Panting, he nudged the toe of his boot under Buckhampton's shoulder and rolled him over. The man's eyes stared up, glazed and sightless.

Was he dead? Right now, Larraby didn't consciously care, even though deep down the dread formed that the British capitalist's death would run his neck into an even tighter noose than the one Marshal Vince Addams had knotted for him, making him not only an outlaw but a murderer with a bounty on his head.

He never got the time to reflect on a walk to the gallows or a life on the dodge.

Several high-pitched screams, like quavering Indian war-cries, split the night from close at hand.

Julia called out a warning. 'Our horses, Tod!'

Instantly there was a pandemonium of whinnying and hammering hoofs, and surging from the shadows at a mad gallop and trampling through the camp came the horses.

They were badly panicked. They were their own horses, and there were only five. But swirling, flashing, snorting, they seemed to fill the whole space between the camp fire and the brush shelter.

Bedrolls and pots and pans were scattered by the churning iron shoes.

Larraby grabbed at a halter and managed to redirect a beast that looked set to pound over Buckhampton's prostrate form.

He failed to fight down the animal's panic and it tore free from the nerveless grasp of his bruised hand and disappeared, clattering and crashing into the darkness of the trees with the rest of them – a blind, loco mob.

Larraby went a short way in pursuit, into a sort of natural alley between the pine trunks. But the horses were going like the Devil himself was chasing them. They smashed through low limbs and undergrowth in a way that brought Larraby's heart to his mouth. Finally, he slipped and fell on the thick layering of slippery pine needles and gave up the futile chase.

'Someone cut them loose an' spooked them into a stampede. I think I saw a knife slash on one bronc's flank,' he told Julia when he'd limped back.

Julia looked around at the encircling darkness and shivered. 'Are there hostiles out there?'

'I think not. There are no Indian troubles hereabouts, an' night is not when they'd choose to attack.'

'So what do we do?'

Larraby dragged the Winchester repeating rifle from the boot alongside his hoof-battered saddle rig.

'The horses are gone for now, but some of them'll maybe return to camp of their own accord by morning. However, somewhere around here is the sonofabitch to blame, an' I mean to get him!'

Julia didn't think that sounded at all safe, but she was learning Larraby was a man who took nothing lying down, and it would be far less safer to let their unknown enemy skulk around them unchallenged in the night.

Plenty mad, Larraby lurched at a run toward the adjacent hollow where he thought the horses had been safely quartered. The moon was bright enough for him to see the flattened grass where the horses had grazed, and the tracks they had made in their wild burst away from their tormentor.

He put down the Winchester and picked up a length of rope – one of the hobbles. It had been cut cleanly with a sharp blade.

A prickling sensation at the back of his neck told him he was being watched. He stiffened, aware that in his eagerness he'd gotten himself unhealthily placed, totally without cover. If whoever had interfered with their horses meant them to die, a bullet could end his life any second.

Had it been stupid to come back here when the unknown would be expecting them to chase the horses?

Larraby decided not. If the intention had been to back-shoot him or the Buckhamptons, that could have been accomplished right off, without touching the horses. The opportunities must have been many since they'd pitched camp, especially while he and Buckhampton had been engrossed in their fight.

Larraby's straining ears caught a pad-padding sound like fast-moving footfalls. From somewhere behind the rimrock of the hollow, metal jingled and stretching leather creaked, tiny sounds borne on the night breeze.

He snatched up the Winchester and loped up the slope.

A horse emerged suddenly into his view as he crested the rim. It was a dappled pony spurred into an urgent gallop, and it went away from him down the far slope, hitting the dim trail beyond in a thunder of hoofs and rising dust.

The rider wore fringed buckskin and a broad-brimmed black sombrero, and Larraby remembered the shadowy figure he'd glimpsed stalking them earlier. One and the same, for sure.

Here was whoever had loosed and stampeded their horses, leaving them afoot, possibly to perish in the wilderness. Without compunction, Larraby threw up the stock of the Winchester to his shoulder and worked the lever, lifting a cartridge into the barrel. He squeezed the trigger and the rifle flashed and crashed.

The dying echo was punctuated by a squeal from the fleeing pony.

'Got you!' Larraby declared in grim exultation.

Through the drifting puff of gunsmoke, he saw the stricken animal stagger on some yards before its legs folded up and it went down in a rolling heap.

The rider baled out of the saddle, dropping to the ground in a lithe leap and crouching behind the pony's dying bulk, as though in expectation of a further rifle shot. Larraby saw no gunbelt or saddle gun, and he figured the fellow would be feeling pretty sick at having had the tables turned on him so completely.

Larraby streaked in on him, rifle presented at waist height. 'Hold it right there, mister! You an' I've got talking to do!'

The crouching figure disregarded the Winchester and leaped at him. So sure was Larraby that the drop he had on his quarry would be respected, he was taken unprepared. Instead of shooting down his assailant at point-blank range, he dropped the rifle and found himself grappling hand to hand.

A knife blade glinted, sharpened on both sides at the tip to a vicious point. Larraby ducked and chopped hard at the wrist behind it. His assailant dropped the weapon with a shriek of agony, but ploughed on.

Larraby registered that the body pitched boldly against him was strangely soft and yielding, and oddly familiar. Then their struggle tipped up the broad brim of the black sombrero.

'Flame!' he cried as moonlight fell on a bronze face with high cheekbones and a smooth jawline.

The shock of recognition caused him to

drop his guard. She slapped him hard, raking his face with her fingernails.

'Yes – Flame, damn you! Sneaking lawdog!' Her voice was full of contempt and fury. 'I hate you and your English pigs!'

Dizzy though he was with surprise and the sting of her blow, Larraby hung on to the scratching, biting woman.

'Why?' he asked, trying to work it out. 'What fired you up to trail us and stampede our horses?'

'What business is that of yours?' she spat back.

11

Fatal Dalliance

Larraby was forced to march Flame back to the camp site in an arm lock. She fought every dragging step of the way.

'What the hell have you got against us, Flame?' he demanded again. 'What was eating on you?'

The black sombrero had been dislodged and hung by its chinstrap at her back. The long tresses of jet-black hair swirled wildly across her face as she shook her head.

'Don't question me, white bastard. I tell you nothing!' She launched into such a stream of savage and obscene invective that Larraby decided it was best they should tie her up and gag her before she did more damage to them or herself.

Julia hastened to fetch the ropes Flame had slashed from their horses' fetlocks.

'A real civilized lady, ain't you?' Larraby said acidly. He could guess that she'd found out they were in quest of Johnny Lord. More than that, he could guess that she was acting in her own behalf to stop them reaching her worthless beau, figuring they meant him harm.

But the way she had and was behaving, he was damned if he was going to try to put her mind at rest. His face was bloody, his head ached and he'd had a bellyful.

She could spend the night trussed up and cooling off. It would give her time, too, to recognize the stupidity of leaving them all without mounts in this desolate country.

'You don't get away with this,' he growled.

She bared her teeth in a snarl. 'Before this is over with, I'll see you dead!'

She struggled with such ferocity that the buckskin was ripped from her shoulder, exposing an expanse of bronze skin from her neck to her heaving breast.

She also bit the back of Larraby's tender-knuckled hand.

'My God, that's more'n enough!' he said. He got her in a hugging grip and clamped a palm over her mouth, pinching her nose between thumb and finger at the same time.

Starved of air, she threshed frantically for several moments, but then her senses blackened and she lost consciousness.

Meanwhile, Lord Buckhampton, who had returned to his own senses many moments back, was playing a wily game. The beating he'd taken from Larraby and the subsequent stampede, of which he'd observed the latter part, had sobered him to a degree of reason where he was able to bring cold calculation to bear in the stead of fiery rage.

When Flame was brought to the spot, yelling and cussing, he made no move to intervene. Let Larraby and his wife handle their violent captive. If she got free, he would look to his own safety then.

And what a magnificent handful the half-breed woman was!

Buckhampton witnessed through slitted eyes and buzzing ears the making of threat and counter-threat. He was forced to swallow painfully and licked his bruised lips when the top half of Flame's well-developed torso was about stripped.

He couldn't be too badly hurt, he figured. Not with the direction his thoughts were going and given the involuntary physical responses he felt himself undergoing. Larraby had done his best and near-killed him but, by hell, he was bloody tough.

That 'breed had the hottest eyes he'd ever seen, and the longest, blackest lashes. She was all-woman and full of fight – an Amazon, but with the breasts in abundant, delicious evidence!

His mind ran in many directions, assembling his needs and desires into a pattern where they might all be accommodated and his enemies routed. He despised Larraby and his prissy wife with her icy, hypocritical censure. He could see they were united against him. But he no longer cared that

Julia was lost to him. Not now he'd seen this fiery part-Indian woman with the dusky skin and dark expressive eyes.

If he didn't lose his head, he could whip Larraby and his mewling wife yet – and at the same time satisfy his lust to possess the exciting newcomer.

Julia returned with the ropes and gasped when she saw Flame senseless.

'Oh, Tod!' she cried, her cheeks draining of colour. 'You haven't killed her?'

'No, she'll be all right,' Larraby assured her. 'The wildcat was getting out of hand an' needed some rough restraining, I'm afraid.' Flame moaned and stirred. 'Here, let's get those ropes fixed before she starts over!'

Larraby pulled Flame's slim wrists behind her back and bound them together, knotting the rope securely.

'What will we do with her?' Julia asked.

'I haven't figured that out yet, but she can't be trusted loose in her present state of mind.'

He took another rope from Julia and moved around to her ankles where he repeated the binding exercise.

'We'd better gag her, too. Else she'll be hollering an' carrying on all night an' I think we could use some sleep.'

In fact, he was bone-tired and the various hurts to his body ached abominably. He went and dug a bandana from his saddle bag, which he quickly folded and tied tightly across Flame's slack mouth.

'Now I think we can safely get ourselves that shuteye,' he suggested.

Julia nodded toward her husband, who was still playing possum, though they didn't know it. 'What about *him?*'

'Throw a blanket over the skunk. He'll be fit for nothing when he comes around, what with the liquor he's guzzled an' the hiding he's taken.'

Larraby's gaze followed the tall, elegant Englishwoman with the soft, lovely skin and golden curls. He found her strangely attractive, despite her foreignness to this untamed landscape and everything in his own background.

Was he in love with her, or she with him? Although she had come to him and shared his hotel bed in her distress, he dismissed that idea instantly. They were unlikely lovers.

For Julia's sake alone, he hoped Buckhampton never found out that they had lain together, joined in a too-brief night of mutual, illicit release.

Julia was a woman bemused by her circumstances, a lost soul seeking solace he had freely given. Maybe he shouldn't have, because he'd wanted no part in interfering in the powerful Lord Buckhampton's affairs. Nor had he wanted any part of this crazy trek into the mountains. But both things, it seemed, had been forced upon him.

Tonight he'd gone up against the English lord with a vengeance.

'I hope he'll give you no trouble,' Julia said in a small voice as she covered her husband in a way that suggested she abhorred even touching him.

Buckhampton feigned a snore.

'I'm sorry he attacked you,' Julia said to Larraby.

'It was none of your fault. He was drunk.'

Impulsively, Julia got up and kissed him full on the lips. 'Thank you, Tod, for everything.'

Larraby shook out his own bedroll, reflecting what an ill-matched couple the Buckhamptons were. It seemed a shame, her married to such an ugly brute – like putting a blood mare with a Mexican jack. But he had to get it back into his mind it was none of his business. He must tread carefully, watching his own interests.

And he'd have to keep on denying to Buckhampton he had designs on his wife and hope he was believed.

Have designs… Hell, he didn't, did he?

Forcefully, he flung the knife he'd taken off Flame into the sod beside his sleeping place. The blade buried itself to the brass handguard. But it did nothing to relieve his tensions.

Lord Buckhampton felt curiously unmoved when his wife kissed Larraby. He didn't give a damn anymore what she did. The whole of his interest where a woman was concerned had been turned in an exhilaratingly fresh direction.

The spirited half-breed prisoner had captivated him. Her liquid brown eyes gleamed so defiantly. Glimpses of rounded bronze flesh were exposed to him in tantalizing flashes through the tatters of ripped buckskin. Delectable! Frisky! What a novel joy it would be to tame and ride such a piece!

He didn't know it, but Flame's charms had affected him in much the same profound way as they once had his wastrel son. In no small part, he'd taken leave of his senses and wouldn't get them back till he'd catered to his obsession.

But he did realize he had to be patient and lay off for a spell, while Larraby and his wife settled to sleep. That wasn't all bad. Though he was as wily as a fox, he felt considerably like a fox that had been run down by a horse and savaged by dogs. He had to lick his wounds.

As he anticipated, it wasn't long before his weary companions showed signs of sound sleep. The only movement came from the trussed prisoner, who wriggled ineffectively in her bonds.

Silent as a wraith from a grave, he rose up and crossed close to where Larraby lay. He pulled Flame's bowie knife out of the soft earth and debated with himself whether to yield to the temptation to plunge it into the sleeping form. But he had to be sensible. Sobered up, he conceded his need of Larraby's services over-ruled other considerations – for the present.

Circling the sleeping guide, he moved to the half-breed woman, a leering grin splitting his hideously blotched face.

A chilly ripple of fear ran along Flame's spine and she ceased her struggles instantly. Her wide eyes fastened on the sharp blade of the bowie knife that she'd carried here herself.

Buckhampton chuckled quietly. The stir of his desire was like fire in his veins.

'Don't you fret, my dear,' he whispered. 'I mean you no harm. You and I are going to take a little walk. If you're good to me, I'll see to it you get no more trouble from that big ruffian.' He pointed toward Larraby with the knife.

His whiskey-sour breath was drawn in by Flame's flaring nostrils. She gagged against the damp cloth of the bandana, but contrived to nod agreeably, relieved to learn she didn't face instant death at the hands of this foreign madman.

If she read the familiar look in his fever-bright eyes aright, he wanted something other than her life. He wanted her like all men did, for the pleasures of her body.

He hacked inexpertly at the rope around her ankles, nicking the skin. But the knife was keen as a razor and the tightness of the bond had numbed her; she felt no great pain.

The rope was finally severed. With a grunt

of satisfaction, Buckhampton seized her tied wrists and pulled her up and after him on stumbling feet. 'Come,' he rasped sharply.

He took her into the trees, away from the camp. When he'd found a place that seemed to suit him, he pushed her down onto the soft pine needles and began tugging at the bandana gag. 'No screaming out,' he warned with an evil glint in his eyes. 'Or, by God, you'll be sorry.'

She shrugged in a gesture of resignation, keeping all hint of emotion out of her face.

Buckhampton tore free the gag and pulled her to him, seeking her mouth hungrily with his own damaged lips.

Hardened though Flame was to unspeakable treatment, the foulness of his breath made her feel quite nauseous. She nearly retched, but managed to pull her mouth free and lurched to her feet.

'What about my hands?' she asked urgently, covering up. She didn't dare offend him. To give the true reason for her resistance to his attentions would be to throw away a chance of freedom – maybe even her life.

'All in good time,' he said thickly. 'I know what I'm doing.' Then he yanked open the remnants of coat and shirt, baring her breasts. The chill night air instantly distended her nipples and she bit back a cry of shock.

He laughed with gloating triumph. 'What I say always goes … see?'

'I guess so,' she said appeasingly.

She forced her mind into the detached state in which she sometimes was forced to entertain the more unsavoury of parlour house clients, and let him begin fumbling with her belt.

He swore as he broke his fingernails on the buckle with his clumsy, ineffectual tugs.

'Here, I can do it,' she murmured through clenched teeth. 'Quick – untie my hands!'

'Yes … yes!' he concurred, snatching up the knife and sawing at the rope.

She snapped the last strands before he was done with the knife, and massaged her chafed wrists and flexed her fingers.

'Hurry it up, woman,' Buckhampton urged

with panting harshness. 'Hell, I'll slice the goddamned britches open with this knife if I have to!'

As she started to ease the snug buckskin pants down over the swell of her thighs, Buckhampton threw aside the knife and unbuttoned his own trousers.

Flame timed it just perfectly, knowing she'd get only the one right moment to act.

Buckhampton's bulging eyes were fixed on the dark, shadowed patch sliding alluringly into view below the taut curve of her abdomen. She lunged forward, tripping him backwards in the tangle of his falling trousers. Then she swooped on the fallen bowie knife.

Without a second of hesitation or mercy, she thrust the wicked nine-inch blade to the haft in his soft naked belly, and ripped upward with all her strength.

'Go to the devils of hell, you filthy pig!'

12

The Hideout

Tod Larraby jerked to his elbow, six-gun in hand and cocked before he was fully awake. A thousand aches racked his sore body, but they were rapidly reduced to numbness by the potently chilling scream that had awakened him and was now repeated.

It was like waking not from, but to a nightmare. Larraby had never heard a human voice raised in such an extremity of terror and agony, not even in wartime when he'd been forced to witness some horrifying atrocities.

His eyes darted round the shadows of their camp. He noted with baffled surprise that Lord Buckhampton and Flame were both missing from the places where they'd been bedded down. His heart lurched and he jumped to his feet, looking to the brush shelter he'd built for Lady Buckhampton.

To his enormous relief, she appeared at its opening.

'Tod! What is it? A bear? A mountain cat?'

'No, Julia. A man, I think.' His voice was a dry croak, as grim as he felt.

Julia saw that her husband and their bound prisoner were gone. She froze, her face milk-white in the moonlight. 'Ralph … the native woman … where have they gone?' she faltered.

Larraby tugged the Winchester from where it had rested with his saddle under his sleeping head. 'Here, take this and get back in the shelter. I'll go find out.'

'Oh, Tod, be careful!'

More sobbing cries rang out from the pines and echoed eerily through the cold, clear night. Julia shuddered and reluctantly did as she was bid.

It was well she did. When Larraby came upon her husband, it was not a pretty sight.

'God!' he groaned, gaping at the huddled man, clutching his spilled intestines. 'He's like to disembowelled!'

Buckhampton was in terminal trauma and was weeping like a distraught child. Larraby didn't know whether he was even aware anyone had come. 'Bitch! Harlot! Jade! Cut me open like a ripe melon. I'm dying, *dying…*'

He pitched over onto his side and rolled, gurgling his last tortured breaths.

Larraby looked all around but saw no sign of Flame. Clearly she'd hightailed it, and now she would keep on going, probably to whatever sanctuary she could find with her precious Johnny Lord.

The irony of it struck him then, but there was no laughter in it. It was too black for that. Out of some undoubtedly mistaken reasoning, and without knowing his identity, Flame had killed the doting father of her lover.

It was cold even under the sheltering trees, but Larraby wiped his sweating brow with the back of his hand. 'She sure as hell must've suckered the old goat, the savage she-varmint.'

He trudged back to the camp to break the news to Julia that her husband had cashed in his chips. When light came, he would have ugly work, returning to do what he could to clean up and recover Buckhampton's corpse. He hoped the scent of blood and death did not bring wolves, though it was happily not the season for such scavenging.

Flame rode wearily northward into an increasingly monotonous wasteland of bleak and dangerous mountainside scarred with deep canyons. The one stroke of good fortune was that she'd been able to round up for herself a horse.

It was the gunfighter's bay which she found cropping the grass in a fertile bottom. He'd allowed her to mount and ride him bareback, but though he was of above-average intelligence and never once bucked, the ride was uncomfortable and she was without food or extra clothing.

She'd never been to the Camp, and it proved as difficult to locate as reputed. She spent the rest of the night and most of the next morning roaming the desolate country. More than once she took vague false trails that were no more than the tracks beaten by foraging bears and descended to dead ends in cherry groves.

When she was despairing of finding sign of human habitation, two riders surged out from a thicket of blue spruce and accosted her.

One of them was Quincy Dunkin, a gaunt, wild-eyed hardcase she'd once met in Leadville and knew was a wanted man who'd thrown in his lot with Jet Konaskis.

'Jest where d'you think you're goin', ma'am?' he asked. His toneless voice showed none of the surprise he must have felt at coming across the lone, raggedly-clad woman.

A wide grin creased the other outlaw's face at the provocative sight of her.

'I'm looking for my friend Johnny Lord,' Flame said. 'He's at the Camp. I figure you boys might be heading that way. Where else would a rider go in this godforsaken place?'

'You're Johnny's woman, eh? Say, I disremember … but have I seen you someplace before?'

'In Leadville, Mr Dunkin. At a bordello.'

The second outlaw snickered at her bold reply. 'Waal, she's plenty feisty, Quincy, an' a whole lot more besides. What say we let her ride on in with us? If Johnny don't want her comp'ny, I guess it'd be a pleasure to *oblige* her our ownselfs!'

Dunkin gave a surly frown. 'Ain't Lord that has the sayso, Chet. That'd be a gent called Konaskis.'

'We won't let her be no trouble,' Chet argued.

'You bet your sweet ass we won't. Konaskis can be real touchy. I seen him up an' salivate a hombre fer less than woman trouble. You gotta watch yourself at the Camp. Ain't no one as fast as the boss, an' I seen him grab his guns over 'bout nothin' a-tall.'

But the grumpy Dunkin and the smirking Chet took the risk and escorted their unexpected find to the notorious outlaw hideout.

The Camp was reached by riding in the bed of a stream. Red-specked trout ran in the bright, swift flow. It was the only practical entrance, Chet said. If Flame decided to leave the stronghold later, and Jet Konaskis said it wasn't allowed, she could forget about it. He jerked a stained thumb upwards at the rocky face overhanging the narrow pass. 'The lookout's manned permanent by a sentry with a sixteen-shot Henry repeater.'

The rift opened up into a secluded, mountain-ringed park. A strip of meadow, about a mile long, sloped up from the stream where beavers had dammed it, creating a pond. Beyond it, the small valley twisted away into greenish-black primaeval forest, an unsurveyed, unexplored tract overshadowed by a soaring face of pinkish granite capped by everlasting snow.

Nestled on the grassy slope was a huddle of rough and ready log cabins and sheds. The best of them were chinked with mud and lime and had stone chimneys. There was a corral and stable; also some cultivated land where corn grew, likely as feed for the horses.

Dunkin and Chet took her to a long, low bunkhouse, their riding boots tramping heavily on a crudely boarded floor.

'Hey, Johnny Lord – look what we've brought yuh!'

'Sweet Jesus! It's Flame!'

The English hell-raiser tossed aside an orange-covered dime novel and swung his legs off his bunk. 'What are you doing here, my pretty wench?'

He was a clean-shaven, amazingly well-groomed young man in a silk shirt that was still mostly white, and well-cut trousers of black whipcord tucked into the tops of tooled leather boots.

But caught unawares, the lines of his aristocratic face seemed already marked by dissipation, and the laugh that brought a lilt to his exclamation didn't ring true. His ebullience was contrived; his rakish charm a sham. His eyes were as cold as a snake's.

These latter things were all beneath Flame's notice. She'd never seen beyond his wealth, his swagger and his lust by which she could manipulate him.

'Johnny, I had to come!' she said earnestly.

Lord pouted. 'Didn't I specifically advise you not to do that?'

'And I have not forgotten, my love, but it was very necessary. To warn you!'

'*Warn* me? Oh, I say, what kind of balderdash is this, darling?'

'A horrible Englishman and his grand wife are looking for you. They came into the mountains. He was a very angry, violent man, but I have killed him.'

'You've *what?*'

'Killed him. With a knife.'

Lord gulped, and Dunkin and Chet were suddenly listening avidly.

The young delinquent laughed weakly.

'Well, I didn't know that I had any English enemies in America, but if you've already killed him, I guess it's all right then.'

'No! There is another man. Very brave, very strong. He is a gunfighter, I am sure, and he was travelling with them. Their guide, it was said. But he asked me many questions and I fear he might be a federal lawman.'

'Good God! You haven't ratted on me to the authorities, have you?'

'I – er – spoke with him. But I never suspected then he might be a US deputy. He was dressed like a saddle bum… I meant no harm, Johnny!'

Lord stifled his dismay and forced himself to smile. Much as he appreciated Flame for her natural talents, he had, as always, to look to his own skin first. He was holed up here on Jet Konaskis' sufferance. And the outlaw king did not look kindly on fugitives who brought the law to his rocky doorstep.

Lord was also aware that every word of his exchange with Flame was being overheard by Quincy Dunkin and Chet Pierce. They were agog.

Flame had behaved damned foolishly, it seemed, talking to an undercover officer and running after him here. He wondered which of his victims in England had come complaining to the American law agencies.

But that didn't greatly matter for now. The wise thing to do would be to go directly to Konaskis and make a clean breast of everything, before he got the sorry tale from his henchmen.

He clapped a fawn sombrero with a snakeskin band at a jaunty angle on his handsome head. He clasped Flame's yielding hand in his own manicured and beringed fingers, and headed for the door.

'Come! We must go along and present you at the court of the famous chief, precious. I wager he'll be most interested in your story.'

Flame felt the weariness that had oppressed her since the tussle with Tod Larraby slipping away from her like an unwanted heavy garment. She loved to hear Johnny Lord's quaint talk, and didn't sense the undercurrents. After a miserable journey through rugged country, she felt like someone who was being welcomed home.

It was not long before she was disabused.

Konaskis' cabin, fittingly, was the Camp's finest, but it was still rough and comfortless by Lord's pampered tastes. Heated by a blackened stove, it was chokingly stuffy with a smell like sweat-stained old clothes. The single large room, with a dirty sheet for a partition, had a long deal table, two benches and some wooden stools. Worn and broken saddle gear and an assortment of firearms cluttered the dark corners.

Konaskis sat in a high-backed chair that had threadbare cushions through which the stuffing poked. He sucked at a long clay pipe, the like of which Flame had never seen before. Even seated, he was clearly a giant of a man. Physical power was the complement of the power endowed by his position as the outlaws' supremo. He had stringy black hair to his shoulders and a chest-length beard to match. A harelip contributed to his frightening ugliness.

He fulfilled the promise of every scaring story Flame had ever heard told of him. He *looked* evil. A real mean brute, with big, wicked ideas.

He listened carefully to Johnny Lord's babble – and all the while undressed Flame with his eyes, which burned with an increasingly intense light, till he looked like some religious fanatic.

But there was nothing religious about the stream of profanity that spewed from his deformed lips when Lord had finished telling Flame's story.

He slammed a fist on the table. 'You stupid bastard, Lord!' he bellowed. 'You told this 'breed whore where you was headed?'

Flame flinched, scared that any moment he would grab out one of the big twin Colts holstered on his belt and blast them to Kingdom Come.

Lord replied, 'Sure, Jet, but I never thought she'd–'

'You never thought at all! That's what you

mean, you poor fool! You let your balls rule your dumb head and had to boast to her – a dime-a-minute trollop no better than a thousand others in a hundred cribs!'

'She's not that cheap and she's no slouch at it…' Lord murmured, trying to look suitably remorseful.

'So you'd have this country crawlin' with tinstars to git inside her drawers ag'in!'

'It wasn't my idea she should follow here,' Lord said stoutly. 'And remember, I've brought you other things, like the schedule for the silver shipments out of my father's mine at Silver Leaf. Surely the train robbery will stretch to payment for eliminating a few nosey dicks?'

'Huh!' Konaskis scoffed. 'I'm countin' on that loot anyhow. It's payin' your keep.'

Flame cringed. She saw that she'd gotten her Johnny into bad trouble. Maybe she could offer herself as compensation? Konaskis was hideous. He was a bully. He frightened her. But for Johnny she would do many things.

She stepped forward, forcing herself to smile at the beast. 'I could be very nice to you, Mr Konaskis. I could warm your bed all night. For nothing.'

Konaskis roared with unexpected laughter. 'We don't need any more of your kind here, slut! Didn't your Johnny tell you? The Camp keeps a seraglio of wild and willin' 'breed girls no diff'rent in the dark from yourself. *I* allocate their services, and I ain't interested in samplin' yourn.'

Flame was affronted. 'Perhaps you would prefer a milksop white woman, Mr Konaskis,' she said disdainfully.

Konaskis took her scornful suggestion seriously. 'Why, mebbe I would at that, 'breed…'

His words set Flame's calculating mind working in a new direction.

'These enemies whose Johnny's mistake has brought into the mountains, they include such a woman – from England, a gentlewoman, you understand? Very lovely. Maybe it will be no big effort for you to round them up after all.'

Konaskis tugged at his beard, his eyes narrowing thoughtfully. Then he laughed again. To Flame's relief it was an agreeable guffaw.

'Yeah! Putting it to an English lady tickles my fancy at that. Could be this jade o' yourn has gotten some ideas in her head after all, Lord…' Konaskis reflected on it. 'A roll in the hay with a genu-ine, international society dame could be a dainty side dish to reward me for the trouble I'm gonna have to take in your behalf, thickhead!'

He laughed again in huge enjoyment of the pleasant prospect.

Even Johnny Lord and Flame, who were no angels, were repulsed.

13

Trouble on the Backtrail

Larraby said, 'We can't bury your husband out here, Julia. We'll have to tote his body back to Silver Leaf.'

Julia looked away from him, hanging her head as though ashamed about what she wanted to say. 'There's no call to indulge in any sentimentality for my sake. He was hateful to me, and unseemly though it may sound, I'm glad he's dead!'

'It ain't that,' Larraby said with a sigh. 'It's a case of self-preservation. The law's not up to much in this region, but Marshal Addams an' others may find our story kinda hard to swallow if'n we show up without him.'

'We'll tell them the truth!'

'Sure, an' we'll let them see the evidence

for themselves, so's they'll have more'n my word I ain't just back-shot Lord Buckhampton someplace. I've tried hard, but I've got a rep, Julia, a notoriety – call it the outlaw brand – and frontier justice ain't what you'd be accustomed to. It has a habit of abdicating its responsibilities to revolvers and lynch ropes!'

Only two of their scattered horses had drifted back to camp in the morning. Larraby thought the others might be trying to wend their way back to the stables in Silver Leaf.

Under other circumstances, he would have gladly deposited Buckhampton's corpse in a shallow grave under the pine needles. That or left him to the wild beasts eventually to tear apart. Then they could have had a mount apiece. As it was, they were to ride double on Julia's mare, and the other horse, a pack animal, would carry essential clothing and bedrolls, plus Buckhampton's mutilated carcass lashed across its back.

They were forced to dump most of their

supplies and gear, keeping only a quantity of biscuits and jerky and two rawhide canteens filled from the sparkling stream that fed the lake by their night-camp.

Again, they went many miles without encountering anyone, retracing the dim trail they'd ridden the day before. But of necessity they made slow progress. Larraby got down frequently, walking for a great part of the warm morning, in order to spare the horse.

They had wearily crested a bald-topped knoll in the mid-afternoon heat when Larraby happened to turn and look back.

'Hellfire! A bunch of riders – an' coming up fast!'

Julia followed his astonished gaze. The dust whipped up under the hoofs of the party's horses made it impossible to figure out who or what they might be.

'Do you think they've seen us?' she asked.

'Must have! It ain't my style to run an' hide, Julia, but we wouldn't have a show trying it.'

‘Who can they be?’

Larraby had a bleak idea. The only sizeable band of inhabitants in these parts was the hidden community of flotsam ruled by Jet Konaskis.

‘Owlhoots, I dare say! We’ll throw ourselves on their mercy an’ find out.’

‘I think I’d prefer to ride on.’

Larraby shrugged. He could appreciate her sentiment, even if he was not in accord with it. ‘All right, but we can’t out-ride them.’

The pursuing bunch dogged their footsteps, much as Larraby expected. Then a rifle cracked, sending a shower of rock splinters from a trailside boulder into their faces. The fragments stung cruelly.

‘Haul up, folks!’ a rough voice yelled. ‘You ain’t hot-footin’ it no place!’

‘Slim chance of that, mister,’ Larraby called laconically.

There were five of the horsemen and they circled round the pair, taking due note of the pack animal’s grisly burden, though their faces remained impassive. A corpse was of no account to hardcases like these. They didn't shout and exclaim, and they had a grim economy about their movements.

Larraby returned stare for cold stare. 'I know you,' he told the one with the smoking rifle, looking into his pock-marked face. 'You're Quincy Dunkin.'

'No less, Mr Larraby, ol' pard,' Dunkin said with a lip-curling sneer. 'An' what brings you inta this country? I'd've thought they woulda strung up a Reb like you long since!'

Larraby nodded curtly. 'Three things, Dunkin,' he said slowly. 'I'm no pard of yours and wouldn't care to be – I seen the things you done to innocent people. Second, they ain't hanged me but it's no thanks to you. Lastly, my business here ain't none of yours!'

Dunkin spurred his horse alongside the bay, reversed the rifle so its barrel was in his hands and clubbed Larraby with it brutally. 'None o' the lip, Larraby!'

Julia cried out as Larraby reeled and

toppled heavily to the hard ground. 'You low thug! How dare you?'

The outlaws sniggered at her outrage.

'Aw, it was jest a gentle tap, ma'am,' Dunkin said. 'It ain't nothin' to what'll be comin' to him unless he changes his tune real fast.'

Larraby staggered to his feet. The scratches inflicted by the bear's swipe were reopened and dripping blood. 'You'd better keep out of this, Julia … say nothing, do what they say.'

'That's good advice, Larraby. You won't neither get nowheres by actin' fresh. You're gonna ride along with us, see?'

'Hell, Quincy,' one of the other ruffians said peevishly, 'let's bump the sassy bastard off. Then we could have ourselfs a good time with the dame.'

'Settle down, man,' Dunkin warned. 'This ain't our party – yet. The boss is mighty desperate to have words with the both of these birds. An' afterwards, if Larraby wants a fight, he's my meat. I'll be just waitin' to tear 'im to pieces!'

His impatient comrade scowled. 'If that's how it sizes up, I'll be first in line fer the woman.' He licked his lips. 'If Konaskis ain't ruint her, thet is! The horny ol' devil don't go easy on breakin' in a woman. He treats 'em like buckin' broncs – them with lots of git-up-an'-go to 'em he leaves fair torn an' bleedin'!'

'Shut up, Clay – you're makin' the lady look kinda faint.' Dunkin turned to Larraby and gestured. 'Give us your gun an' get up behind her, an' make sure there's no monkey business. We've wasted enough time chewin' the fat.'

Larraby sized up the situation. It was five to two – no worse, because if Julia hadn't been here, he might have been free to make some purely reckless play.

He sighed bitterly. They had no option but to go along with this degenerate gang.

They were the most helpless of prisoners, and their outlook was demoralisingly black.

Dusk was coming on fast when Quincy Dunkin led his small band toward the untidy cluster of buildings that was the nucleus of the Camp. Word sizzled round the place like wildfire. Men jabbered excitedly when they came out to watch. The few women – many half-breeds and none Anglo-Saxon – cackled. Much of the talk was lewd. Tod Larraby they took as just another of their own class. But the refined Lady Buckhampton they acknowledged as altogether different.

Julia sat the saddle with golden head hanging and both hands clutching hard upon the brass pommel.

'She's too handsome to be *good,'* one of the haggard-looking women opined, her words audible to the captives. Her companions chortled. Larraby glared murderously as he steadied Julia's weakly swaying form.

Dunkin said, 'Watch it, Larraby! Don't let your hands git too attached to her. She ain't your property no more. Konaskis has sole rights to all women here till he says otherwise, y'unnerstand?'

Whatever scrap of lingering respect Larraby may have had for his wartime co-fighter vanished like frost in the sun. The anger blazed within him.

'I'll watch it, Dunkin,' he said, and jerked his head at the rubbernecking rabble. 'But who's going to watch them?'

'Don't bother your head none 'bout that, Larraby. We're takin' you on into the chief directly.'

Dunkin led his troop up to the best-set of the dismal-looking log structures that managed to bring a touch of squalor to the sunset-gold grandeur of the park.

'Jet Konaskis!' Dunkin hailed. 'Hi, boss! Jet!'

The imposing figure of the black-bearded outlaw king appeared at the door of the cabin.

'These here's our guests, Jet,' Dunkin said. 'Kinda ornery when we grabbed 'em, but me an' the fellers got 'em quieted down. The guy's a troublemaker called Larraby.'

'Climb on down, Larraby,' Konaskis

ordered curtly. 'That there's a mighty fine-lookin' woman.' He sneered at Larraby's dishevelled clothes and bloody head. 'Too purty fer a broken-down bum to be ridin' double with, I reck'n.'

Larraby scowled, but dismounted, wondering bitterly if he should have made the stand against Dunkin and his four partners after all.

Suicide on the mountain slopes could have been better than what Konaskis might have in store for them here. Maybe they would have died cleanly without having to suffer whatever humiliation and violation Konaskis and his devil's crew had in mind.

'That's better,' Konaskis rumbled, eyeing Julia lasciviously. 'Did you ever see a finer-lookin' body on a full-grown white woman?'

His dirty thoughts were transparent. He ran his hot gaze up from her trim ankles, tracing the long line of her legs through the stretched fabric of her riding-dress, lingering at her rounded bosom and resting finally on her exquisite face with its creamy skin and china-blue eyes. 'With tits like yourn yuh'd make a good milker, ma'am,' he mocked.

Julia tossed her head, colouring and looking away from him. Larraby felt for her. She'd already tolerated the embarrassing taunts and foul language of Dunkin and company during the ride here. In most frontier communities, even the roughest of men moderated their profanity in the presence of women. But decency and morality were forgotten to this caste of cut-throats and desperadoes.

Konaskis laughed. 'Yeah, a real high-toned looker, sure 'nough. Help her down, Quincy, an' bring 'em on in.'

Dunkin needed no further bidding. He swung off his mount and rushed to comply, hands pawing eagerly as he pulled Julia roughly from the saddle.

Larraby could stand no more. He surged forward, laying a hand on Dunkin's shoulder. 'I can't have you–'

He was restrained instantly. At a nod from Konaskis and a flick of his finger, two of

Dunkin's fellow-riders grabbed Larraby and dragged him back without ceremony.

'This ain't your roost, Larraby,' Konaskis said. 'Long as the lady's on my place, I'll decide the things she needs help in, yuh savvy?'

Larraby's arms were locked. Defiantly, he said, 'This land is public domain, Konaskis.'

'Yeah, I s'pose it is at that,' Konaskis purred. 'So I c'n do as I like anyhow!'

'I didn't say the lady was public property,' Larraby said coldly. 'Unhand her, Dunkin. She's capable of deciding for herself whether she wants to go into that dump, without no help from you.'

Konaskis laughed scornfully. 'Yuh're takin' too much on yuhself, mister. Yuh can shuck the fool idea yuh gonna git any choices around here.'

He stepped forward and struck the impotent Larraby brutally in the face with his fist. 'Mebbe yuh'll make a nice punchin' bag!'

Larraby groaned insensibly, supported on

his feet only by the efforts of Dunkin's side-kicks.

'You swine!' Julia cried. 'What are you going to do to us?'

'Yuh'll find out,' jeered Konaskis. 'Let's have 'em inside, you men. Treat 'em rough as you like – nothin's barred!'

With the sunset reddening the mountain tops, Johnny Lord had taken Flame with him upstream, beyond the beaver workings, to seek privacy in the violet gloom of the cottonwoods and aspens that crowded the river's banks.

Tucked away in the trees, in a small, man-cleared dell, were the remains of a shack, built there by a long-gone trapper in the days before the park had been appropriated by Konaskis and his wild bunch. Stretchers on which the trapper had dried the beaver skins still leaned against the decaying walls, now damp and moss-grown in the new shade of regenerating forest.

Johnny Lord and others had put the hovel

to like uses before, with one and sometimes more of the Camp women. But these were raddled and shop-worn drabs, formerly from town cribs. Abandoned by their pimps, they had drifted to this last outpost of humanity where their pitiful lives could be extended by devotion to the comfort and diversion of men who could not be choosy.

Now Lord had the exciting woman who most inflamed his debauched tastes.

He dug into a pocket and produced a match. The sulphur tip scratched against his long thumbnail and flared into a blue-orange flame, which he applied to the wick of a shadeless lamp standing on a three-legged table propped up by a crate. Flickering light created great looming shadows.

Flame had done her stuff for Johnny in more comfortable surroundings – like plushy, mirrored bordellos – but the drawling Englishman with his roguish ways delighted her as none other did, and she had no complaints at regaining his amorous attentions.

She threw her arms around him, pressing

herself up against him tightly. 'It's been too long, Johnny … take me,' she whispered.

Lord was more than willing to oblige her, right there and then on a bug-eaten old blanket on the dirt floor. Responding hungrily to her entreaties, he did everything she desired. And after being away from her, it seemed better than ever; more intense.

But he had more than the consolations of the flesh on his mind.

'Happy?' he murmured with a boyish grin, after he was emptied and had withdrawn from her and rolled onto his back.

'Oh, yes, Johnny,' she said, sitting up, the long black hair swirling round her shoulders and abundant breasts. 'I'm so happy to have saved you from that disgusting English pig I stuck with my knife. Was he one of the old fools you bested in the London gaming saloons?' She laughed wickedly and slapped the top of his bare leg. 'Or have you been big, too, inside his prim young wife?'

It was – more or less – the question Lord had been asking himself. He pulled himself up behind her, wrapped his arms around her perspiring nakedness and buried his face in her hair.

'I don't know, Flame. *Who* was he? Didn't you hear the bastard's name?'

She frowned, trying to remember the gossiping voices on the streets of Silver Leaf.

'They said he was an earl…' she mused. 'From Buck-someplace…'

Lord's fondling hands suddenly stilled and dropped from her, causing her to shiver.

'Good God Almighty! The name wasn't *Buckhampton*, was it?'

14

Larraby Gets a Break

Johnny Lord tugged on his clothes with uncommonly careless haste and rushed from the trapper's shack, leaving Flame perplexed and hurt. A dread suspicion – almost a sick certainty – tugged at his racing heart.

The manhunter and lecher his lover had stabbed to a gruesome death was the Guv'nor ... his own despotic sire!

He burst out of the trees and saw the group of horses and people dispersing from the patch of trampled turf fronting Konaskis' cabin. He recognised all but two of the animals as the mounts ridden by Quincy Dunkin and his crowd.

One of the unfamiliar animals carried a

corpse. Could this be the man Flame had killed?

Two of the outlaws taking a more sordid interest in the gruesome load were unlashing it and pulling it from the pack animal's back. The curious looked on with a hushed fascination.

Lord's fears were confirmed. The processes of decomposition were already disfiguring the dead man's facial features and the corpse stank, despite the coolness and thinness of the mountain air. But it was unmistakably and shockingly his father.

'Shit!' he exclaimed, his face ashen. 'Where are the people with whom Dunkin brought this in?'

The spark of decency still in him was being fanned into urgent life.

A head was nodded in the direction of Konaskis' cabin. The story had gone the rounds quickly. 'The lawhound and the woman you wronged in England are with the boss. You ain't got nothin' to be a-feared about no more, Johnny!'

'You're all deluded by lies!' Lord announced, wild-eyed, his voice cracking. 'The woman is my stepmother, and the man no law officer but an agent of my father's!'

He span on his heel, lurched to the door of the cabin like a terrified steer prodded to the slaughter, and thrust it open.

Konaskis was seated in his chair. Tod Larraby and Julia, ringed by Dunkin and three other hardcases, stood before him, their expressions grim and strained in the light from the lamp that hung from the rafters.

'Jet!' Lord blurted. 'You'll have to let these folk go. There's been the most godawful bloomer.'

'Bloomer?' Konaskis' face darkened angrily at the Englishman's interruption of his inquisition of the captives.

'Lord John!' Julia exclaimed. 'Please – you must save us from this horrible man!'

Lord ignored her, but pressed his remarkable argument to Konaskis.

'I mean, it's all a bloody mistake! You can't

hold this woman – she's my stepmother and can do me no harm. And the man, I fancy, is not a marshal – merely a hireling of my old man.'

Konaskis scoffed openly.

'To hell with your fancy lingo, kid! That's some tale yuh're pitchin' me. 'Sides, I got this woman as fair pickin's fer gettin' the bastards offa yore back, remember?'

'No! You can't have her!'

'You wanna watch me? Put her on the table, fellers!'

Larraby roared and kicked and struggled against Dunkin and the other man holding him. 'You're crazy, Konaskis! Listen to the kid!'

The chips were down and Johnny Lord rushed forward to take on the two men manhandling Julia in a desperate attempt to redeem himself.

Before Larraby knew what was happening, the room seemed filled with a milling free-for-all. Konaskis sprang to his feet with a speed surprising for so bulky a man. His ham-like fist cuffed Lord to the floor.

Behind him, Larraby heard the door open again and a second female voice was added shrilly to the cries.

'Johnny!'

Larraby saw Johnny Lord roll on the boards and snatch a stubby Derringer from a sneak holster somewhere at his back. Konaskis was charging forward to stomp Lord with his heavy boots.

It was at the precise moment Lord fired that a fleet figure threw itself between the two men to thwart Konaskis' brutal assault. At close quarters, Flame stopped the .45 slug intended for Konaskis.

Without another scream, she fell instantly dead – whereupon Konaskis hauled his six-gun from the leather and shot Lord in the head before he could master his blank dismay and squeeze a second shot from the Derringer.

The two shots were ear-splitting in the confined space of the cabin and gunsmoke added its reek to the fetid atmosphere.

Larraby's custodians were stunned by the rapidity and confusion of events. Their grip loosened and they stared in stupid surprise, giving Larraby all the break he needed.

He wrenched himself free, twisting violently and suddenly. He arched himself on the twist, so when Dunkin threw a swinging punch with a startled yell, he was able to seize the arm that whistled over his head.

Dropping to his knee, Larraby used all the remaining strength in his own arms, legs and body, plus the outlaw's powerful momentum, to jerk the arm down like a lever and send Dunkin somersaulting on.

Dunkin was hurled into Konaskis at the level of his groin. Konaskis doubled up with a yelp, the shooter clattered from his grasp and the two men crumpled in a heavy tangle to the floorboards. The crash shook the building. It also shoved the deal table back against the wall, and brought the sheet hung as a partition down on top of them.

The men holding Julia were agape. Julia

sank her teeth into the back of a hand and managed to knee the other man squelchingly in the crotch.

Larraby dealt the bitten man a ferocious rabbit-punch which felled him unconscious, if not dead or crippled for life. The other man turned yellow and backed off, pleading incoherently for mercy. Larraby was showing none. He grabbed up Konaskis' chair by its high back and swung it, knocking the agonised man down in a senseless heap.

'Get out, Julia!' Larraby barked, arming himself with a Colt from the man he had rabbit-punched. 'Get out quick!'

Julia jumped toward the door, Larraby at her heels.

Larraby pointed. 'To the corral! Unless we can grab horses, we'll get nowhere!'

The shots and the sounds of fighting had caused less amazement outside than strangers might have expected. In the half-light, it was several moments before the idlers recognised the fleeing figures were those of Dunkin's prisoners. Then they rushed first to

Konaskis' cabin.

Larraby saw his own reliable bay in the corral. At a whistle, the horse came across to him obediently. He had no saddle, but a pile of gear lay in an untidy heap by the pole fence. Larraby pushed his hand against the bay's rump and manoeuvred him sideways into position over a saddle he dragged out from the heap. He stooped and seized the saddle's horn, heaving it up and over the horse's back in a jingling arc.

Still no pursuit. 'We've caught 'em flat-footed!' he jubilated to Julia.

He reached under the bay's belly for the cinch, lacing the latigo straps through the ring.

There was no nicety in his next urgent movements. He caught Julia up bodily and just about threw her into the saddle. 'Head out the way we came in,' he ordered. 'But don't try to get past the sentry. Wait for me before you get there.'

Then he slapped the horse on the rump and it went away like a racehorse from the starting gate.

The shooting started as Julia flashed past Konaskis' cabin. It was led off by Konaskis himself, who let rip with a scattergun from the doorway. But the bay was moving fast and he hadn't taken aim. The hail of shot from the twin-barrelled Remington 10-gauge missed the target, and horse and rider were out of range before Konaskis could fire a second load.

'That was only the woman!' he roared. 'Where's Larraby?'

Larraby, now mounted himself on a high-standing chestnut, gave him his answer. He snapped a shot at Konaskis with the purloined Colt. The lead was not entirely wasted since it forced the outlaw chief to duck back into cover, which gave Larraby the chance to storm past.

But he didn't push the horse hard for long and had settled to an easy canter before he met up with Julia in the first clump of trees, where she'd pulled off to the side of the rough trail.

'They were shooting!' she exclaimed. 'We must ride like the wind!'

Larraby shook his head. 'That's what we let them do! Nothing saps the strength an' wind of a horse so much as to run it suddenly at full speed before it gets a chance to warm up with work – specially in the mountains where the air is cold.'

He led them deeper into the trees, squeezing between thick trunks that the stirrups scraped bark from on both sides.

Minutes later, a posse of outlaws hurtled past back of them, their horses' hoofs pounding the trail and their wild howls fracturing the night like a human wolf pack.

Larraby dismounted and slipped speedily through the timber, parallel to the trail, till he was as close as it was possible to get to the narrow pass that was the gateway to Konaskis' lawless kingdom.

He overheard the end of an angry exchange of shouts between Konaskis and his sentry.

'Yuh musta see'd 'em. They was goin' hell

fer leather! Yuh bin asleep, yuh stupid bastard!'

'I didn't let no one sneak past me, Jet!' the sentry whined, but the incredulous pursuers shouted him down. Their adamancy made him less than certain sure himself that stealthy riders hadn't slipped by him in the dark depths below.

He mounted his own bronc, and clattered down a tricky staircase of rocks to join them. The trust among riffraff was scant. If the quarries were found, he didn't want to find out about it when Konaskis despatched a man to return and shoot him in the back. 'Passel o' damned coyotes,' he grumbled to himself.

After the bunch had ridden off pell-mell in supposed pursuit, Larraby went back to Julia.

'C'mon,' he said. 'Now's the time to get through the pass and make ourselves scarce in the mountains. Once we're out of this hole-in-the-wall, there's no way they'll catch us. I know how to cover tracks, an' there'll never be enough of 'em to search the whole terrain.'

The journey back to the mining region was tough. The circuitous route they took involved four days of hard riding. Larraby relied on the sun and stars to keep them going in the right direction, though many times they were forced to turn back by great, impassable gulches and retrace the steps of hours.

They lived off the land for food. Larraby shot a rabbit, and trout populated the streams. They also came across the stomach of a bear with a cupful of cherrystones in it, which they broke open for the kernals.

Without blankets and extra clothing, the cold nights brought them to an intimacy neither saw reason to obstruct.

But as they drew closer to Silver Leaf, Larraby came to the decision he had consciously been putting off.

'It's no use, Julia. I daren't return with you to that place, or any other come to that.

Marshal Addams trapped me into working for your husband an' he isn't about to accept what happened to him on our sayso. I've got a past – a record, though I swear it's the best part undeserved.'

His words drew a searching look from Julia. 'Where will you go then?' she asked.

He shrugged, granite-faced. 'Over the mountains again. To Wyoming … Utah … California. I don't know. Does it matter? I guess I'll just keep on running till I get somewhere folks'll give an old Reb a chance.'

Julia broke her gaze and looked away.

Larraby believed it took a talent he didn't have to figure out what women were thinking. But he saw her beautiful blue eyes were filling with tears.

'Tod, it matters to me,' she said. 'You're different from any man I've ever met, and I'll never be able to forget you. Can't I come with you?'

Larraby squeezed her hand. 'No, Julia, it has to be goodbye. I've no life to offer a lady – always drifting, looking over my shoulder.

I've no home or position to give you, an' no knowing if I'd safely be allowed to come back to them if I had.'

'But I don't need those things, Tod!' she protested fervently. 'I want to be with you always, very much. If you don't let me come, I'll always be wondering, always worrying what danger you might be in. You must let me stay by your side. I know we could make it work. *You* know we could!'

'Well, maybe we could…' he conceded with a strange weakness, his emotions in a turmoil.

And even as he spoke, he knew he was accepting she had the strength and courage to stand by him. She'd made her choice, just as she had that evening she'd come to his room in the hotel at Silver Leaf. He knew she was right. Bizarre though it looked on the surface, they were right together and there was no going separate ways now, for either of them.

She delved into a cunningly cut pocket in her riding-dress.

'We will travel together, my dear outlaw,' she said determinedly. 'I love you with my whole heart and can trust my happiness to you. Here, I have rolls of money tucked away which I took from Ralph's bags. We will buy tickets and ride the great Pacific railroad. We will escape to San Francisco – maybe board ship to foreign lands, to a paradise in the South Seas!'

Larraby knew then that somewhere along the trail he'd learned to love her as he'd never loved a woman before, and that everything she said was true. He didn't answer in words to what she proposed, but pulled her close into his arms and claimed the kiss that waited for him on her softly parted lips.

She sighed contentedly. 'It's all settled then,' she said.

But less than twenty-four hours later it didn't seem likely they would ever see the new life they dreamed of. Nor any life at all.

15

Showdown with Konaskis

When bullion was shipped from Silver Leaf, it was taken on the first stage of its journey by the narrow-gauge railroad to Denver. Responsibility for its transportation was assumed by the express agents Wells, Fargo & Co., whose name appeared in gold lettering on the train's purpose-built car.

For extra security, two guards were locked in behind the car's steel-reinforced doors in Silver Leaf to protect the consignment, and the key was carried to Denver by special messenger for delivery to the city's Wells Fargo agent, whose duty it was to meet the train, release the guards and arrange the bullion's further movement.

The special messenger went by swift horse

across country that did not allow for the carriage of heavy goods. Leastways, that was what always happened right up to the day the messenger was struck down by the incapacitating malady known as the shakes, or simply 'the fever', and was in fact acute malaria.

Then Marshal Vince Addams, told of the problem, took it on himself to deliver the key to Denver. It was outside the range of his obligations, but the vicissitudes of a Western town-tamer's life had taught him a thing or two. It did no harm to curry favour with the mining bosses who owned most of Silver Leaf, and it might stand him in good stead should he ever need seek employment with Wells Fargo.

Addams, a town lawman, was no horseman. Therefore, he decided he would take what he thought was the small risk of riding along on the train itself.

The three-car train that drew into the depot at Silver Leaf was already partly filled from its earlier halt at an upline town which was a fashionable mountain resort in summer. When Addams supervised the loading of the bullion car, and the locking-up of the guards, he had an audience which included Tod Larraby and Lady Buckhampton, who had boarded at the previous stop.

The fugitive lovers' apprehension became alarm as the familiar black-moustached, hard-faced marshal, his apparent escort duties completed, proceeded to climb the iron steps into their own car.

'Damnit! We're boxed. He's sure to notice us before we reach Denver,' Larraby whispered harshly.

Julia clutched his hand. 'Come,' she said urgently. 'We'll step out onto the rear platform.'

As Addams entered at one end of the long saloon, they left at the other. Up front, the big brass locomotive bell clanged and the train jerked out of Silver Leaf under a belch of black smoke and hissing steam.

Denver was not on a transcontinental route, but Larraby and Julia could switch there to the Denver Pacific line into Wyoming, where they could connect with the Union Pacific and go west.

The view from the platform was inspiring in every sense, except for providing the solution to Larraby's and Julia's problem – how to dodge Vince Addams.

The building of the railroad had been a marvel of engineering. The tracks threaded through a steep canyon, along ledges blasted and excavated out of the rock. The canyon's sides had been stripped of timber cover by the voracious mining industry, except where the walls were near-perpendicular and stunted pines and cedars had been left to cling to precarious life.

'It'd be no good leaving the train here, even if it slowed,' Larraby said, assessing the desolate scene.

'I've ridden this train before, with Lord Buckhampton,' Julia told him. 'The track descends a steep, curving grade onto a kind of causeway of stones built atop the creek bed, then it runs into a stretch covered by snow-sheds. If the train were to stop there, we could jump and slip away through the trees along the creek.'

Larraby's eyes took on a gleam. '*If* the train stops... Julia, I'll *make* it stop! And soon as it does, you gotta quit this deck an' hide. They may chase me, but not far, I figure. When the train goes on, I'll come back an' find you.'

'What in the world – where are you going?' Julia asked, a sick knot of concern forming in her stomach. She was bewildered by his sudden change of mood and rapped orders.

But Larraby was no longer beside her. He was over the back rail and climbing the ladder to the car roof.

Eyes narrowed against the slipstream, which was filled with choking smoke and flying cinders from the loco, Larraby crawled along the cleated roofs of the swaying cars.

Eventually, he reached the loco's tender and leaped from the last car onto the stacked two-foot lengths of wood used for fuel. The Colt was in his fist as he scrambled forward.

The fireman saw him first as he turned from the open firebox. 'Hell, mister, what kinda joke is this?' he said, staring straight into the black muzzle of a six-shooter.

'It ain't a joke an' it ain't a robbery!' Larraby snapped back. 'Hoist your hands!'

The fireman obeyed, but the engineer let go his throttle and grabbed a wrench.

Larraby fired, the bullet hitting the wrench and hurling it from the engineer's numbed hand. 'You made me do that,' he growled. 'Just stop the train afore the snowsheds an' nobody don't get hurt!'

Looking sick, the engineer shoved in the throttle and jerked on the shining brass brake levers. He also kicked the sandbox lever, releasing grit onto the track in front of each drive wheel, assisting their purchase on the iron rails.

'That's better,' Larraby grunted.

The loco was rounding a steep downhill curve and shuddering into a clanking crawl as it traversed the causeway built up on the creek bed. The fireman, leaning out the cab, gave a sudden yell.

'What d'yuh mean, it ain't no hold-up? You're a liar! Someone's done sabotaged the damned way. Pards o'your'n, mister!'

The railroad men Larraby was covering glared at him accusingly.

Larraby briefly took his eyes off them and glanced ahead himself. Just before the tracks vanished under the weathered grey timber of the snow-sheds, they'd been substantially undermined by what looked like the results of a washout … or blasting.

The iron rails were twisted and buckled and the wooden ties splintered. If the train had hit the damaged section at full tilt, it would have been derailed and toppled down the embankment into the creek.

'Ain't none o' my business, gents,' Larraby responded indignantly. 'Stands to reason … why would I've stopped the train if you was meant to tip into a mess of rocks like that? I guess I've saved your lives!'

'Then who the hell–?' the engineer began. He never finished the question.

Suddenly, riding from the shadows of the snow-sheds, came a bunch of horsemen, whooping and yelling and firing guns in the air. They wore masks, but Larraby had no trouble recognizing the imposing Jet Konaskis and the eager Quincy Dunkin among the frontrunners.

Konaskis was livid. 'The sonsofbitches are gonna stop – there ain't gonna be no wreck!' he told Dunkin moments earlier.

'I don't get it It's almost like they's bin tipped off,' Dunkin said balefully.

Konaskis spat. 'Too bad if'n they is. Ain't gonna be nothin' to signify.' He dragged a package from his saddle-bag. 'It's only the Wells Fargo guys we gotta worry about, an' we brung more dynamite to blast open that bullion car like a sardine can!'

Neither Dunkin nor any others of the waiting gang had the slightest urge to contradict their bloodthirsty leader. But Konaskis' summation of the state of affairs did not prove entirely correct. After they had broken cover, emerging from the mouth of the snow-sheds, the first indication they were going to meet opposition came from the rear passenger car.

Vince Addams, forced to show his salt in defence of the alarmed citizenry riding the train, leaned out a window and replied to the outlaws' intimidating fire.

Shots from the loopholes in the walls of the bullion car, the outlaws had been expecting, but this caught them unawares.

Addams hit an outlaw's horse. It lost its footing and crashed into the shallows of the creek, spilling its rider and rolling on him. The flowing stream was stained pink and the horse, which failed to rise, thrashed the water, squealing.

Addams was emboldened. He leaned out to try to repeat the stunt and pick off another of the ambushing gunmen. He was cherishing an illusion in thinking it could be so easy a second time.

It was his last mistake.

'Let 'im have it!' Konaskis roared.

Several aimed guns barked flame, and the slugs ploughed into Addams' chest and head. For a few fleeting seconds the lawman's widened eyes beamed shock and the fear of death.

Then they glazed and he slumped forward from the waist. His muscles relinquished their hold on life; his body toppled slowly through the window, spraying blood down the side of the car from his multiple wounds.

'Jest like shootin' fish in a barrel!' an outlaw jeered triumphantly.

Meanwhile, Larraby, crouched in the tender's cargo of wood, hadn't been observed by the outlaws, who were below him, splashing along the creek bed adjacent to the causeway.

Larraby swore softly under his breath, hoping Julia would have the good sense to stay on the train now shooting had broken out.

He couldn't feel sorry for Addams. He had been just another conniving tinstar. Put under pressure, real pressure, he had gone to pieces, made a fool play and paid for it and all his other crimes.

'Goddamn murderers!' the engineer spluttered with barely suppressed rage. 'If yuh ain't with 'em, mister, how come yuh ain't shootin' back with thet hog-leg in yore paw?'

Larraby laughed without mirth. 'No point in going off half-cock. That's what the marshal just done, an' got himself killed. I can see it all from up here – an' I'm saving my bullets till I know I can make 'em count!'

Most of the passengers aboard the train had been tourists. They and the train's conductor wanted no part in heroics. The shooting died out, though its echoes rang through the canyon and puffs of gunsmoke drifted on the cool mountain breeze.

Unopposed, Konaskis, Dunkin and a few others dismounted and moved in on the bullion car, covered by their sidekicks. They crouched low, beneath the level of the loopholes in the car's steel-panelled sides and began climbing the sides of the embankment, finding easy hand- and footholds in the chinks between the piled rocks.

'This is gonna be easy. The guards are trapped in there,' Konaskis said. 'They can't get a bead on us through them goddamn silly gun slits, an' they can't get out.'

'Sure, Jet, an' we'll open it up for 'em with the dynamite. Talk about make monkeys outa them!'

Konaskis laughed with cruel contempt. 'More like ground beef, Quincy!'

Something akin to fear sent a shiver down Larraby's spine. Dynamite would not only blast open the bullion car. It would probably wreck the connected cars, too, killing many of the innocent people aboard ... maybe Julia.

It was time to show his hand.

Larraby bobbed up quickly. He steadied the Colt on his left forearm, picking his target – the ominous cluster of short-fused dynamite sticks Konaskis gripped in one hand.

He was seen immediately. The outlaws on horseback along the creek bed yelled warnings to Konaskis and Dunkin. Some with quicker reactions fired at Larraby. But most had already spent the shells in their hardware and not gotten around to emptying and recharging the chambers.

That may have saved his life; certainly it allowed him to fulfil his daring intention.

With slugs humming past him like angry hornets, Larraby let the hammer of his own Colt fall.

Booom!

Simultaneously with the kick and blast of the handgun, a deafening explosion thundered in front of Larraby, and a shot from the creek bed tore upwards through his left shoulder. The man-made slope to the creekbed – the whole embankment – disappeared in a great geyser of flame and debris.

The canyon trembled to the concussion and the train rocked.

Out of the swirling smoke and dust, rocks, big and small, began to rain down.

The roar of the dynamite was still sounding in Larraby's ears. He was down on the stacked wood, his left arm weak and useless, sticky with blood.

Hanging dust dimmed the light in the canyon, blocking out the sun for long moments – but as it began to clear, Larraby registered that Jet Konaskis and Quincy Dunkin had vanished, though a few tatters of clothing and some unrecognizable lumps had been dispersed amongst the shattered fragments of rock around the stark, black crater now existing where he'd last seen them.

Farther along the creek, the mounted remnants of Konaskis' gang were beating a retreat. Others, dazed and on foot, were struggling in the same direction. Yet others, mortally wounded by the blast, were dying hard in the shallows of the creek, along with their fallen horses.

Larraby was wondering at his own consciousness when a weakness overtook him and swallowed him up in blackness.

Julia's words came to Larraby as though her voice was ringing in some distant, fog-damp cave.

But she was right beside him, cradling him in her arms. 'You've got to be all right, Tod!' she pleaded. 'For God's sake and mine, you must live. We'll get you to a doctor. You can't die! I need you … this country needs you! You've saved these people from a horrible death. Your story will be told throughout America, and you'll be rightly greeted as a hero.'

Julia was right, of course. Tod Larraby was no longer to be treated as a renegade. He was redeemed. Very shortly, his praises were going to be sung all over the West, and he would be glorified back East, too.

For that was one of the peculiarities which characterized the narrow band of time that went down in history as the Wild West. Even as the frontier heroes – Wild Bill Hickock, Buffalo Bill Cody, Pat Garrett and the rest – performed their adventurous deeds, their legends were being told in their own lifetimes in print and on stage, suitably embellished by the newspaper, dime novel and playwright hacks to create America's own enduring mythology.

But for now rehabilitation lay in the future, and the Reb who'd been branded an outlaw was content to be in the loving arms of his lady.

'Are you plumb crazy, Julia?' Larraby croaked. 'I'm bone-tired and I'm bloodied, but I ain't going to die. I've got just too much to live for!'

The publishers hope that this book has given you enjoyable reading. Large Print Books are especially designed to be as easy to see and hold as possible. If you wish a complete list of our books please ask at your local library or write directly to:

Dales Large Print Books
Magna House, Long Preston,
Skipton, North Yorkshire.
BD23 4ND